Walk in the Light
While There Is
Light

Leo
Tolstoy

Walk in the Light
While There Is
Light

Compiled by Lawrence Jordan

Fleming H. Revell
A Division of Baker Book House Co
Grand Rapids, Michigan 49516

© 2001 by Morning Star Rising, Inc.

Published by Fleming H. Revell
a division of Baker Book House Company
P.O. Box 6287, Grand Rapids, MI 49516-6287

Printed in the United States of America

Library of Congress Cataloging-in-Publication Data

Tolstoy, Leo, graf, 1828–1910.
   [Short stories. English. Selections]
   Walk in the light while there is light / Leo Tolstoy ; compiled by Lawrence Jordan.
      p.   cm.
   Contents: Walk in the light while there is light—The long exile—Little girls wiser than their elders.
   ISBN 0-8007-1782-1 (cloth)
   1. Tolstoy, Leo, graf, 1828–1910—Translations into English. I. Jordan, Lawrence. II. Title.
PG3366.A13J58   2001
891.73'3—dc21   2001019701

For current information about all releases from Baker Book House, visit our web site:
http://www.bakerbooks.com

Contents

5

Acknowledgments

o one writes a book alone. And no compiler, not even one compiling the rich written legacy of Leo Tolstoy, works alone. I wish to acknowledge the immeasurable contributions others have made to this project, and to my life, by sharing freely of their time, their resources, and their encouragement.

All of the stories in this collection were translated by Nathan Haskell Dole, and all unascribed footnotes are by the translator.

I am extremely grateful and indebted to Lonnie Hull DuPont, my extraordinary editor who has stewarded these stories through many a twist and turn, and whose idea it was to do a series of the stories. Thank you, Lonnie.

I am also indebted to Patricia Williams, who read the first collection of stories, found my telephone number and e-mail address, and persistently insisted that I do something about making the stories available again.

Thanks to Chinita, Danai, and Noel Jr., the three pointers in my life whose presence keeps me walking toward the light.

And finally, I am profoundly grateful and deeply indebted to Leo Tolstoy, servant of the Most High, who preserved for us in these writings golden morsels of the Truth. It is my sincere desire that many people will benefit from the ideas contained in these stories, come to know the saving knowledge of Jesus Christ, and pass that knowledge, and this book, on to others.

Introduction

Only one thing is needful—the law of love which brings the highest happiness to every individual as well as to all mankind.

Leo Tolstoy

On a winter Sunday afternoon in 1992, I walked into a storefront schoolroom in Brooklyn, New York, to listen as a gifted Christian actress read stories to children and their parents.

Hearing Leo Tolstoy's "Where Love Is, There God Is Also" read aloud that afternoon started me on a personal odyssey with Tolstoy's gospel writings that led to research and discoveries about Tolstoy the man, the artist and his Christ-centered writings. The first part of this odyssey culminated in the publication in 1993 of *Where God Is, There Love Is Also,* a collection of three of Tolstoy's gospel stories. The book won the Evangelical Christian Booksellers Association's Gold Medallion as the best gift book of the year, classic category. More importantly, the book became a blessing to many, many people.

Here is how one reader responded to the book: "Anyone finding themselves intimidated by the works of Tolstoy should start off with reading this book. These three short stories . . . are some of the most powerful words I have seen put to paper. Those troubled by today's problems owe it to themselves to read this book and absorb the relevance that in fact is timeless. Even those . . . [who lack a] belief in God will be moved and question their beliefs. Any of Tolstoy's works are a must read in everyone's lifetime, but these stories remain special to this reader." Scores of other readers—some encountering Tolstoy for the first time, others being exposed to his Christian works for the first time— responded in a similar fashion.

Fleming H. Revell has now published a new edition of *Where Love Is, There God Is Also* as the first book in a series dedicated to Tolstoy's Christ-centered stories. The present volume, *Walk in the Light While There Is Light,* is book two.

The relevance of Tolstoy's life and works for Christians today is discussed at length in the introduction to *Where Love Is, There God Is Also.* Was he a Christian? Are his "gospel" stories Christ-centered works or merely moral tales? And what of his infamous personal behavior? How can that be reconciled with the themes of his stories?

I urge you to read the introduction to *Where Love Is, There God Is Also* for a fuller exploration of these issues. A. N. Wilson's excellent biography, *Tolstoy,* is also a must read for anyone wanting a comprehensive understanding of the man, his times, and his works. But here, in the introduction to this volume, I want to focus on the gift and the Giver, not the man.

The modern Christian world needs to read Tolstoy's gospel stories. They are a great gift to the body of Christ, a splendid, undiscovered part of our heritage.

Though Tolstoy is now widely known throughout the world for his novels, it was his religious writings that first brought him widespread attention in the West. It is largely through his nonfiction "religious" writings that Western readers first encounter Leo Tolstoy. After writing *War and Peace* and *Anna Karenina,* Tolstoy had a personal religious revelation—today we would say that he was "born again." In April 1877 he finished *Anna Karenina*. From that point until the end of his life—for the next thirty-three years—Tolstoy was overwhelmingly preoccupied with the things of the spirit in both his fiction and nonfiction writings.

What makes Tolstoy important for our age is his simplicity and his moral directness. Some Christians do not practice what they preach. What counted most for Tolstoy was the moral and spiritual power of Christ in the lives of men and women. For Tolstoy, the gospel was not merely a preference, something followed out of convenience, but a conviction—truth to be adhered to no matter what, under any and all circumstances, regardless of the consequences, even, yes, even unto death. "Is the moral teaching of Jesus true?" he asks. If so, it demands that we make changes in our lives. To be a Christian, we must live each day in harmony with these teachings.

The stories presented in the first volume of this series highlight the struggles and inconsistencies inherent in the human attempt to live as Christ has directed us to live—to expel anger from our hearts, to turn the other cheek to those who wrong us, to rid ourselves of lust and greed.

The stories in the present volume are a further exploration into the difficulties of the Christian life—a look at the high cost of discipleship, the price of adhering to conviction. But the spiritual rewards of living the Christian life are highlighted as well.

Tolstoy's gospel stories need to be reintroduced to the Christian community and to the general public as inspirational gems. Since these stories have not been available for such a long time, they are like a treasure waiting to be stumbled upon, a pearl of great price waiting to be found. If the stories were better known, especially within the Christian community, they would already be considered classics, for they speak as eloquently today as they did when they were first written in the 1800s. They can and do stand on their own.

The three stories in this volume all speak of the cost of discipleship, how living the gospel with conviction, no matter what the consequences, is the only true path for a Christian.

In "Little Girls Wiser Than Their Elders," written in 1885, two girls get into an argument that threatens to destroy their entire village, pitting hostile adult against hostile adult. But children do not hold grudges. "If ye are not like little children, ye cannot enter into the Kingdom of God."

"The Long Exile," written in 1872, shows us that bad things can happen to good people and that unearned suffering is redemptive—a theme that Gandhi and Martin Luther King Jr. would echo years later. Aksenof, a prosperous young tradesman, is imprisoned for a crime he did not commit and loses everything he has—his wealth, his family, and his health. After spending years in prison, he comes to understand that "no one but God can know the truth, and He is the only one from whom to expect it." When a new prisoner connected to his past arrives, Aksenof must choose between his Christian convictions—his faith—and freedom. He chooses Christ: "And from that time, Askenof ceased to send in petitions, ceased to hope, and only prayed to God." Though he is never released from prison, he dies a free man in Christ, with a "wonderful peace in his soul."

"Walk in the Light While There Is Light," written in 1893, is set in Tarsus, birthplace of the apostle Paul, during the time of the early Christian church. The story is a profound meditation on the necessity of living the Christian life with conviction: "We all profess one law, but our powers of fulfilling it vary in each individual; some have greater, some have less. One has already made great improvement in the good life, while another has only just begun in it. At the head of us all stands Christ, with his life, and we all try to imitate him, and in this only we see our well-being." Two friends take different paths. One chooses the path of Christ; the other takes the worldly path. One is wealthy and privileged; the other materially poor and persecuted for his beliefs—yet he lacks nothing of real value.

In an age that often excuses wrongs for expediency's sake, these stories speak to us with a moral directness that is much needed. There are absolutes. There is good and there is evil in the world. The stories in this book are explorations, a search for moral truths and how these truths play themselves out in human affairs. They will touch and move, challenge and inspire both Christians and non-Christians.

Lawrence Jordan
New York, New York

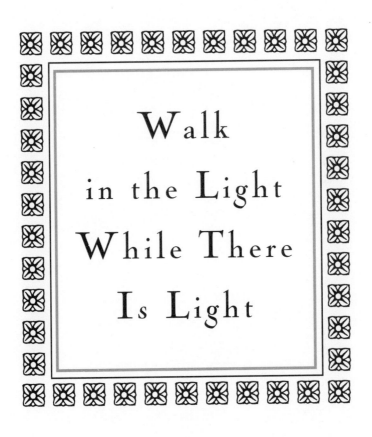

Walk
in the Light
While There
Is Light

A TALE OF THE TIME OF THE EARLY CHRISTIANS

1

It was in the reign of the Roman Emperor Trajan, a century after the birth of Christ. It was at the time when the disciples of Christ's disciples were still living, and the Christians faithfully observed the laws of the Master as it is related in the Acts:

> And the multitude of them that believed were of one heart and of one soul; neither said any of them that aught of the things which he possessed was his own; but they had all things common. And with great power gave the Apostles witness of the resurrection of the Lord Jesus; and great grace was upon them all. Neither was there any among them that lacked; for as many as were possessors of lands or houses sold them and brought the prices of the things that were sold and laid them down at the Apostles' feet; and distribution was made unto every man according as he had need.
>
> Acts 4:32–35

In these early times, a rich Syrian tradesman named Juvenal, a dealer in precious stones, was living in the province of Cilicia, in the city of Tarsus. He was of poor and simple origin; but, by dint of hard work and skill in his art, he had accumulated property and won the respect of his fellow-citizens. He had traveled widely in different lands; and though he was not a literate man, he had seen and learned much, and the city people regarded him highly for his intellect and his probity.

He held to the pagan faith of Rome, which was professed by all respectable people of the Roman Empire—that faith burdened with ceremonies which the emperors since the days of Augustus had so strenuously inculcated, and which the reigning Emperor Trajan so strictly maintained.

The province of Cilicia was far from Rome, but it was administered by a Roman proconsul, and everything that took place in Rome found its echo in Cilicia, and the rulers were mimic emperors.

Juvenal remembered all that had been told him in his childhood about the actions of Nero in Rome. As time went on, he had seen how one emperor after another perished; and, like a clever man, he came to the conclusion that there was nothing sacred about the Roman religion, but that it was all the work of human hands. The senselessness of all the life which went on around him, especially that in Rome, where his business often took him, bewildered him. He had his doubts, he could not comprehend everything; and he attributed this to his lack of cultivation.

He was married, and four children had been born to him; but three had died young, and only one, a son named Julius, survived. Juvenal lavished on this son Julius all his affection and all his care. He especially wished so to educate his son that he might not be tortured by such doubts regarding life as had bewildered him. When Julius had passed the age of fifteen, his father intrusted his education to a philosopher who had settled in their city and devoted himself to the instruction of youth. Juvenal intrusted him to this philosopher, together with a comrade of his, Pamphilius, the son of a former slave whom Juvenal had freed.

The two boys were of the same age, both handsome, and good friends. They studied diligently, and both of them were of good morals. Julius distinguished himself more in the study of the poets and in mathematics; Pamphilius, in the study of philosophy.

About a year before the completion of their course of study, Pamphilius, coming to school one day, explained to the teacher that his widowed mother was going to the city of Daphne, and that he would be obliged to give up his studies.

The teacher was sorry to lose a pupil who had reflected credit on him; Juvenal also was sorry, but sorriest of all was Julius. But in spite of all their entreaties that he should stay and finish his studies, Pamphilius remained obdurate, and after thanking his friends for their love toward him and their solicitude for him, he took his departure.

Two years passed: Julius completed his studies; and during all that time he did not once see his friend.

One day, however, he met him in the street, invited him home, and began to ask him how and where he lived.

Pamphilius told him he still lived in the same place with his mother.

"We do not live alone," said he, "but many friends live with us, and we have all things in common."

"What do you mean 'in common'?" asked Julius.

"In such a way that none of us considers anything his private property."

"Why do you do that way?"

"We are Christians," said Pamphilius.

"Is it possible!" cried Julius. "Why, I have been told that Christians kill children and eat them. Can it be that you take part in doing such things?"

"Come and see," replied Pamphilius. "We do nothing of the sort; we live simply, trying to do nothing wrong."

"But how can you live, if you have no property of your own?"

"We support each other. If we give our brethren our labors, then they give us theirs."

"But if your brethren take your labors and don't reciprocate, then what?"

"We don't have such persons," said Pamphilius; "such persons prefer to live luxuriously, and they don't join us; life among us is simple, and without luxury."

"But are there not many lazy ones who would delight in being fed for nothing?"

"Yes, there are some such, and we willingly receive them. Not long ago a man of that character came to us— a runaway slave; at first, it is true, he was lazy, and led a bad life, but soon he changed his life, and has now become one of the good brethren."

"But supposing he had not ordered his life aright?"

"Well, there are some such. The old man Cyril says that we must treat such as if they were the very best of the brethren, and love them all the more."

"Can one love good-for-nothings?"

"It is impossible to help loving a human being."

"But how can you give all men whatever they ask of you?" asked Julius. "If my father gave all persons whatever they asked him for, very soon he wouldn't have anything left."

"I don't know," replied Pamphilius. "We always have enough left for our necessities. Even if it came about that we had nothing to eat or nothing to wear, then we ask the others and they give to us. Yes, it sometimes happens so. Only once did I ever have to go to bed without my supper, and that was because I was very tired and did not feel like going to ask any of the brethren."

"I don't know how you do," said Julius, "only what my father says: if he didn't have his own property, and if he gave to every one who asked him, he would die of starvation."

"We don't! Come and see. We live, and not only do not lack, but we have even more than we need."

"How can that be?"

"This is the way of it: We all profess one law, but our powers of fulfilling it vary in each individual; some have greater, some have less. One has already made great improvement in the good life, while another has only just begun in it. At the head of us all stands Christ, with His life, and we all try to imitate Him, and in this only we see our well-being. Certain of us, like the old man Cyril and his wife Pelagia, are our leaders; others stand next to them, and still others in a third rank, but all of us are traveling along the same path. Those in advance are already near to the law of Christ—self-renunciation—and they are willing to lose their life in order to save it. These need nothing; they have no regret for themselves, and to those that ask they give their last possession according to the law of Christ. There are others, feebler, who cannot give all they have, who have some pity on themselves, who grow weak if they don't have their usual dress and food, and cannot give everything away. Then there are others still weaker— such as have only just started on the path; these still live in the old way, keeping much for themselves and giving away only what is superfluous. Even these that linger in the rear give aid to those in the van. Moreover, all of us are entangled by our relationships with pagans. One man's father is a pagan and has a property, and gives to his son. The son gives to those that ask, but the father still continues to provide. The mother of another is a pagan, and has pity on her son, and helps him. A third has heathen children, while a mother is a Christian, and the children obey her, give to her, and beg her not to give her possessions away, while she, out of love to them, takes what they give her, and gives to others. Then, again, a fourth will have a pagan wife, and a fifth a pagan husband. Thus all are perplexed, and those in the van would be glad to give their all, but they cannot. In this way the feeble in faith are confirmed, and thus much of the superfluous is collected together."

In reply to this Julius said:

"Well, if this is so, then it means you fail to observe the teaching of Christ and only pretend to observe it. For if you don't give away your all, then there is no distinction between us and you. In my mind, if you are going to be a Christian, then you must fulfil the whole law; give everything away and remain a beggar."

"That is the best way of all," said Pamphilius. "Do so!"

"Yes, I will do so when I see that you do."

"We do not wish to set an example. And I don't advise you to join us and renounce your present life for a mere display; we act as we do, not for show, but as a part of our religion."

"What do you mean—your 'religion'?"

"Why, it means that salvation from the evils of the world, from death, is to be found only in life according to the teaching of Christ. And it makes no difference to us what men say about us. We are not doing this in the eyes of men, but because in this alone do we see life and welfare."

"It is impossible not to live for self," said Julius. "The gods instilled in us our instinct to love ourselves better than others and to seek happiness for ourselves. And you do the same thing. You confess that some of you have pity on yourselves; more and more they will look out for their own pleasures, and be ever more willing to give up your faith and do just what we are doing."

"No," replied Pamphilius; "our brethren will go in another path and will never weaken, but will become more and more confirmed in it: just as a fire will never go out when wood is added to it. In this is our faith."

"I don't find in what this faith consists."

"Our faith is this: that we understand life as Christ has interpreted it to us."

"How is that?"

"Christ uttered some such parable as this: Certain vine-dressers cultivated a vineyard, and they were obliged to pay tribute to the owner of the vineyard. We are the vine-dressers who live in the world and have to pay tribute to God and fulfil His will. But those that held to the worldly faith fancied that the vineyard was theirs, that they had nothing to pay for it, but only to enjoy the fruits of it. The Lord of the vineyard sent a messenger to these men to receive His tribute, but they drove him away. The Lord of the vineyard sent His Son after the tribute, but they killed Him, thinking that after that no one would interfere with them. This is the belief of the world, whereby all men live who do not acknowledge that life is given only for God's service. But Christ has taught us how false is the worldly belief that it would be better for man if he drove out of the vineyard the Master's messenger and His Son and avoided paying tribute, for He showed us that we must either pay tribute or be expelled from the vineyard. He taught us that all pleasures which we call pleasures—eating, drinking, amusements—cannot be pleasures if our life is devoted to them, that they are pleasures only when we seek another—the fulfilment of the will of God; that only then these are pleasures, as a present reward following the fulfilment of the will of God. To wish to have pleasure without the labor of fulfilling the will of God, to separate pleasure from work, is the same as to tear off the stalks of flowers and plant them without seeds. We have this belief, and therefore we cannot seek for deception in place of truth. Our faith consists in this: that the welfare of life is not in its pleasures, but in the fulfilment of the will of God without a thought of its pleasures, or hoping for them. And thus we live, and the longer we live the more we see that pleasure and well-being, like a wheel behind the shafts, follow on the fulfilment of the will of God. Our Lord has said: 'Come unto me all ye that labor and are heavy laden, and I will give you rest! Take my yoke upon you and learn of me, for I am meek and lowly in heart; and ye shall find rest unto your souls, for my yoke is easy and my burden is light.'"

Thus said Pamphilius.

Julius listened, and his heart was stirred within him; but what Pamphilius said was not clear to him: at one moment it seemed to him that Pamphilius was deceiving him, but when he looked into his friend's kindly eyes and remembered his goodness, it seemed to him that Pamphilius was deceiving himself.

Pamphilius invited Julius to visit him so as to examine into the life they led, and if it pleased him to remain and live with them.

And Julius promised, but he did not go to Pamphilius; and being drawn into his own life, he forgot about him.

2

Julius' father was rich, and as he loved his only son and was proud of him, he never stinted him for money. Julius lived the life of rich young men; in idleness, luxury, and dissipated amusements, which have always been, and are still, the same—wine, gambling, and fast women.

But the pleasures to which Julius gave himself up kept demanding more and more money, and after a time he found he had not enough. Once he asked for more than his father generally gave him. His father gave it to him, but accompanied it with a rebuke. The son, conscious that he was to blame, and yet unwilling to acknowledge his fault, became angry, behaved rudely to his father, as those that are aware of their guilt, and are unwilling to confess it, are apt to do.

The money he obtained from his father was very quickly spent, and moreover, about the same time Julius and a companion happened to get into a drunken quarrel, and killed a man. The prefect of the city heard about it, and was desirous of subjecting Julius to punishment, but his father succeeded in bringing about his pardon. At this time, Julius, by his irregular life, required still more money. He borrowed it of a boon companion and agreed to repay it. Moreover his mistress asked him to give her a present; she desired a pearl necklace, and he knew that if he did not accede to her request, she would throw him over and take up with a rich man, who had already for some time been trying to entice her away from Julius.

Julius went to his mother and told her he had got to have some money; that if he did not succeed in raising as much as he needed, he should kill himself. For the fact that he had got into such a scrape he blamed his father, not himself. He said:

"My father has accustomed me to a luxurious life, and then he began to blame me for wanting money. If at first he had given me what I needed without scolding, then with what he gave me afterward I should have regulated my life, and should not have needed much; but as he has always given me too little, I have had to apply to usurers, and they have extorted from me everything I had, and so nothing is left for me to live on, as a rich young man should, and I am put to shame before my companions; and yet my father can't seem to understand this at all. He has forgotten that he was young once himself. He got me into this position, and now, if he does not give me what I ask for, I shall kill myself."

The mother, who spoiled her son, went to his father. The father called the young man, and began to upbraid both him and his mother. The son answered the father rudely. The father struck him. The son seized his father's arm. The father called to his slaves and ordered them to take the young man and lock him up.

When he was left alone, Julius cursed his father and the day he was born. His own death or his father's presented itself before him as the only way of escape from the position in which he found himself.

Julius' mother suffered more than he did. She did not comprehend who was really to blame in all this. She felt nothing but pity for her beloved child. She went to her husband and begged him to forgive the youth, but he refused to listen to her, and began to reproach her for having spoiled her son; she blamed him, and the upshot of it was the husband beat his wife. But the wife made no account of the beating. She went to the son and persuaded him to go and beg his father's forgiveness and yield to his wishes. She promised him, if he would do so, she would give him the money he needed, and not let his father know.

The son consented, and then the mother went to her husband and urged him to pardon the young man. The father for a long time stormed at his wife and son, but at last decided to pardon him, but only on the condition that he should abandon his dissipated life and marry a rich tradesman's daughter, whose father wished her to enter into an engagement with him.

"He shall have money from me and his wife's dowry," said the young man's father, "and then let him enter upon a regular life. If he will agree to fulfil my wishes I will pardon him. But otherwise I will give him nothing, and at his first offense I will deliver him over into the hands of the prefect."

Julius agreed to everything, and was released. He promised to marry and to abandon his wicked ways, but he had no intention of doing so; and life at home now became a perfect hell for him: his father did not speak to him, and was quarreling about him with his mother, who wept.

On the next day his mother called him to her room and secretly gave him a precious stone which she had got from her husband.

"Go, sell it; not here, but in another city, and with the money do what you need, and I will manage to conceal the loss for a time, and if it is discovered I will blame it on one of the slaves."

Julius' heart was touched by his mother's words. He was horror-struck at what she had done; and he left home, but did not take the precious stone with him. He himself did not know where or wherefore he was going. He kept going on and on, away from the city, feeling the necessity of remaining alone, and thinking over all that had happened to him and was before him. As he kept going farther and farther away, he came entirely beyond the city limits and entered a grove sacred to the goddess Diana. Coming to a solitary spot, he began to think.

The first thought that occurred to him was to ask help of the goddess. But he no longer believed in his gods, and so he knew that no help was to be expected from them. But if no help came from them, then who would help him? As he thought over his position, it seemed to him too terrible. His soul was all confusion and gloom.

But there was help for it. He had to appeal to his conscience, and he began to examine into his life and his
acts. And both seemed to him wicked, and, more than
all, stupid. Why was he tormenting himself so? He had
few pleasures, and many trials and tribulations!

The principal thing was that he felt himself all alone.
Hitherto he had had a beloved mother, a father; he certainly had friends; now he had no one. No one loved
him. He was a burden to every one. He had succeeded
in bringing trouble into all their lives: he had caused
his mother to quarrel with his father; he had wasted his
father's substance, gathered with so much labor all his
life long; he had been a dangerous and disagreeable rival
to his friends. There could be no doubt about it—all
would find it a relief if he were dead.

As he reviewed his life, he remembered Pamphilius,
and his last meeting with him, and how Pamphilius had
invited him to come there, to the Christians. And it
occurred to him not to return home, but to go straight
to the Christians, and remain with them.

"But was his position so desperate?" he asked himself,
and again he proceeded to review what had happened,
and again he was horror-struck because no one seemed
to love him, and he loved no one. His mother, father,
friends, did not love him, and must wish he were dead;
but whom did he himself love? His friends? He was conscious that he did not love any one. All were rivals of his,

all were pitiless toward him, now that he was in disgrace. "His father?' he asked himself, and horror seized him when at this question he looked into his heart. Not only did he not love him, but he hated him for his stinginess, for the affront he had put on him. He hated him, and, moreover, he saw plainly that for his own happiness his father's death was essential.

"Yes," Julius asked to himself, "and supposing I knew that no one would see it or ever find it out, what would I do if I could with one blow, once and for all, deprive him of life and set myself free?"

And Julius replied to this question:

"Yes, I should kill him!"

He replied to this question, and was horror-struck at himself.

"My mother? Yes, I pity her, but I do not love her; it makes no difference to me what happens to her—all I need is her help. . . . Yes, I am a wild beast! and a wild beast beaten and tracked to its lair, and the only distinction is that I am able, if I chose, to quit this false, wicked life; I can do what the wild beast cannot—I can kill myself. I hate my father, there is no one I love . . . neither my mother, nor my friends—but how about Pamphilius?"

And again he remembered his one friend. He began to recall the last interview, and their conversation, and Pamphilius' words, how, according to their teaching,

Christ had said: "Come unto me all ye that labor and are heavy laden, and I will give you rest." Can that be true?

As he went on with his thoughts and recollections, he recalled Pamphilius' sweet, joyous, passionless face, and he felt inclined to believe in what Pamphilius said.

"What am I, in reality?" he asked himself. "Who am I? A man seeking well-being. I have sought for it in animal pleasures, and have not found it. And all living beings, like myself, also failed to find it. All are evil, and suffer. If any man is always happy, it is because he is seeking for nothing. He says that there are many such, and that all men will be such if they obey their Master's teachings. What if this is the truth? Whether it is the truth or not, it attracts me to it, and I am going."

Thus said Julius to himself, and he left the grove resolved never again to return home, and he bent his steps to the town where the Christians lived.

3

Julius went on boldly and cheerfully, and the farther he went and the more vividly he represented to himself the life of the Christians, remembering all to himself that Pamphilius had said, the more joyous he became in spirit.

The sun was already descending toward the west, and he felt the need of rest, when he fell in with a man who was resting and taking his nooning. This man was of middle age, and had an intellectual face. He was sitting and eating olives and cakes. When he saw Julius, he smiled and said:

"How are you, young man? The way is still long. Sit down and rest."

Julius thanked him, and sat down.

"Where are you going?" asked the stranger.

"To the Christians," said Julius; and he gave a truthful account of his life and his decision.

The stranger listened attentively, and though he asked him about certain details, he did not express his opinion; but when Julius had finished, the stranger stowed away in his wallet the remains of his luncheon, arranged his attire, and said:

"Young man, do not carry out your intention; you are making a mistake. I know life, and you do not. I know the Christians, and you do not know them. Listen, and I will explain your whole life and your ideas; and when you hear me you shall adopt the decision that seems to you the wiser. You are young, rich, handsome, strong; your passions are boiling in you. You wish to find a quiet refuge in which your passions would not disturb you, and you would not suffer from their consequences; and it seems to you that you might find such a refuge among the Christians.

"There is no such place, my dear young man, because what troubles you is not peculiar to Cilicia or to Rome, but to yourself. In the quiet of a village solitude the same passions will torment you—only a hundred times more violently. The fraud of the Christians, or their mistake—for I don't care to judge them—consists simply in this—that they don't wish to understand the nature of man. The only person who can perfectly carry out their teachings is an old man who has outlived all his passions. A man in his prime, or a youth like you who has not yet learned life or himself, cannot submit to their law, because this law has for its basis, not the nature of man, but an idle philosophy. If you go to them, you will suffer what you suffer now, only in a far higher degree. Now, your passions entice you along false paths; but having once made a mistake in your direction, you can rectify it. Now, you still have the satisfaction of passion freed—in other words—of life.

"But, in their midst, controlling your passions by main force, you will make precisely the same mistakes, if not worse ones; and, besides that suffering, you will also have the incessant anguish of the unsatisfied human longings. Let the water out of a dam, and it will irrigate the soil and the meadows, and quench the thirst of animals; but if you keep it back it will tear away the earth and trickle away in mud. It is the same with the passions. The teachings of the Christians—beyond those doctrines from which they get consolation, and which I will not speak of—their teachings, I say, for life, consist in the following: They do not recognize violence, they do not recognize war or courts of justice, they do not recognize private property, they do not recognize the sciences, the arts, or anything which makes life cheerful and pleasant.

"All this would be good if all men were such as they describe their teacher to have been. But you see this is not so, and cannot be. Men are bad, and given over to their passions. It is this play of passions, and the collisions resulting from them, that keep men in those conditions of life in which they live. The barbarians know no restraint, and one savage, for the satisfaction of his own desires, would destroy the whole world, if all men submitted as these Christians submit. If the gods lodged in the human heart the sentiments of anger, of vengeance, even of evil against evil-doers, they must have done it because these sentiments are necessary for the life of men. The Christians teach that these feelings are wicked, and that men would be happy if they did not have them; there would be no murders, no punishments, no want. That is true; but one might as well take the position that men ought to refrain from eating for the sake of their happiness. In reality, it would put an end to greediness, hunger, and all the misfortunes that come from it. But this supposition could not change the nature of man. Even if two or three dozen people, believing in this, and actually refraining from food, should die of starvation, it would not change the nature of man. The same, exactly, with the other passions of men: indignation, wrath, vengeance, even love for women, for luxury, for splendor and pomp, are characteristic of the gods, and consequently they are the ineradicable characteristics of man.

"Annihilate man's nutrition, and you annihilate man. In exactly the same way annihilate the passions characteristic of man, and you annihilate humanity.

"The same is true also of private property, which the Christian would do away with. Look around you: every vineyard, every inclosure, every house, every ass—everything has been produced by men under the conditions of private property. Abolish the right of private property, and not a vineyard would be planted, not a creature would be trained and pastured. The Christians assure you that they have no rights of private property; but they enjoy its fruits. They say they have all things in common, and everything they have is brought to one place; but what they bring together they receive from men who have private property. They merely deceive men, or in the very best light, deceive themselves. You say they themselves work in order to support life, but the work they do would not support them if they did not take advantage of what men possessing private property produced. Even if they could support themselves, it would be a mere existence, and there would be no place among them for the arts and sciences. [And indeed it is impossible for them to do otherwise. They do not even acknowledge the advantage of our arts and sciences.] All their doctrine tends to reduce them to a primitive condition, to barbarism, to the animal. They cannot serve humanity by arts and sciences, and as they do not know them, they renounce them; they cannot take advantage of the qualities which are the peculiar prerogative of man and ally him to the gods. They will not have temples, or statues, or theaters, or museums. They say these things are not necessary for them. The easiest way not to be ashamed of one's own baseness is to scorn nobility; and this they do. They are atheists. They do not recognize the gods, or their interference in the affairs of men. They acknowledge only the father of their teacher, whom they also call their father, and their teacher himself, who, according to their notions, has revealed to them all the mysteries of life. Their doctrine is a wretched deception.

"Notice one thing—our doctrine asserts that the world depends on the gods; the gods afford protection to men. In order that men may live well, they must reverence the gods, must search and think, and then our lives are regulated on the one hand by the will of the gods, on the other by the collective wisdom of all mankind. We live, think, search, and consequently approve the truth.

"But they have neither the gods nor their wills, nor the wisdom of humanity, but only one thing—a blind faith in their crucified teacher, and in all he said to them.

"Now consider well: which is the more hopeful guide—the will of the gods and the collective, free activity of human wisdom, or the compulsory blind belief in the words of one man?"

Julius was struck by what the stranger said to him, and especially by his last words. Not only was his purpose of going to the Christians shaken, but it now seemed to him strange enough that he, under the influence of his misfortunes, could ever have come to such a foolish decision. But the question still remained, What was he to do now, and how was he to escape from the difficult circumstances in which he was placed, and so, after he had related his situation, he asked the stranger's advice.

"That is the very thing that I wanted to speak about," continued the stranger. "What are you to do? Your way, as far as human wisdom is given me, is clear to me. All your misfortunes are the results of the passions peculiar to men. Passion has seduced you, has led you so far that you have suffered. Such are the ordinary lessons of life. These lessons must be turned to your advantage. You have learned much, and you know what is bitter and what is sweet; you cannot repeat the mistakes you have made. Profit by your experience. What has hurt you more than all is your quarrel with your father; this quarrel is the outcome of your position. Take another, and the quarrel will either cease, or at least it will not be so painfully apparent. All your tribulations have arisen from the irregularity of your position. You have yielded to the gaieties of youth; this was natural, and therefore it was certainly good. It was good while it was appropriate to your age. But that time has passed; you, with the powers of manhood, have yielded to the friskiness of youth, and it was bad. You have now reached the time when you must become a man, a citizen, and serve the state, and work for its welfare. Your father proposes to you to marry. His advice is wise. You have outlived one period of life—your youth—and have reached another. All your tribulations are the indications of a period of transition. Recognize that the period of youth is passed, and having boldly renounced all that belonged to it, and that is not appropriate to manhood, start on your new way. Marry, give up the amusements of youth, occupy yourself with trade, with social affairs, with arts and sciences, and you will find peace and joy as well as reconciliation with your father. The main thing that has disturbed you has been the unnaturalness of your position. Now you have reached manhood, and you must enter into matrimony, and be a man.

"And therefore my chief advice is: Fulfil your father's wishes, and marry. If you are attracted by that solitude which you expected to find among the Christians, if you are inclined toward philosophy and not to the activities of life, you can with profit devote yourself to this only after you have had experience of life in its actuality. But you will know this only as an independent citizen and head of a family. If then you feel drawn to a solitude, yield to it; then it will be a genuine inclination, and not a whim if discontent, as it is now. Then go."

These last words, more than anything else, persuaded Julius. He thanked the stranger, and returned home.

His mother received him joyfully. The father, also, on learning his intention to submit to his will and marry the girl whom he had chosen for him, was reconciled to him.

4

In three months Julius' wedding with the beautiful Eulampia was celebrated, and the young man, having changed his manner of life, began to live with his wife in their own house and to conduct a part of the business which his father intrusted to him.

Once upon a time he went on business to a not very distant city, and there, as he was sitting in a merchant's shop, he saw Pamphilius passing by with a girl whom he did not know. Both were walking, laden with heavy bunches of grapes, which they were selling. Julius, when he recognized his friend, went out to him and asked him to go into the shop and have a talk with him. The young girl, seeing Pamphilius' desire to go with his friend, and his reluctance to leave her alone, hastened to say that she did not need him, and that she would sit down with the grapes and wait for customers. Pamphilius thanked her, and went with Julius into the shop.

Julius asked his acquaintance, the merchant, permission to go with his friend into his private room, and, having received this permission, he went with Pamphilius into the apartment in the rear of the shop.

The friends inquired of each about the circumstances of their lives. Pamphilius' life had not changed since they had last seen each other: he had continued to live in the Christian community, he was not married, and he assured his friend that his life each year, day, and hour had been growing happier and happier.

Julius told his friend all that had happened to him, and how he had started to join the Christians, when his meeting with the stranger had opened his eyes to the mistakes of the Christians, and to his great obligation to marry, and how he had followed his advice and married.

"Well, tell me, are you happy now?" asked Pamphilius. "Have you found in marriage what the stranger promised you?"

"Happy?" repeated Julius. "What is being happy? If you mean by that word full satisfaction of my desires, then of course I am not happy. I am conducting my trade with success, men are beginning to respect me, and in both of these respects I find some satisfaction. Although I see many men who are richer and more regarded than I, yet I foresee the possibility of equaling them and even of excelling them. This side of my life is full; but my marriage, I will say frankly, does not satisfy me. I will say more:

I am conscious that this same marriage, which ought to have given me joy, has not done so, and that the joy I experienced at first has kept growing less and less, and has at last vanished, and in its place, where joy had been, out of marriage arose sorrow. My wife is beautiful, intellectual, well educated, and good. At first I was perfectly happy. But now—this you can't know, having no wife—there have arisen causes of discord between us, at one time because she seeks my caresses when I am indifferent toward her, at another time the case is reversed. Moreover, for love, novelty is necessary. A woman less fascinating than my wife fascinates me more at first, but afterward becomes still less fascinating than my wife. I have already experienced this. No, I have not found satisfaction in matrimony. Yes, my friend," said Julius, in conclusion, "the philosophers are right; life does not give what the soul desires. This I have experienced in my marriage. But the fact that life does not give that happiness which the soul desires does not prove that your fraudulent practices can give it," he added with a smile.

"In what do you see we are fraudulent?" asked Pamphilius.

"Your fraud consists in this: that in order to free men from the evils connected with the facts of life, you repudiate all the facts of life—life itself. In order to free yourselves from disenchantment, you repudiate enchantment, you repudiate marriage itself."

"We do not repudiate marriage," said Pamphilius.

"If not marriage, then you repudiate love."

"On the contrary, we repudiate everything except love. For us it is the chief corner-stone of everything."

"I don't understand you," said Julius. "As far as I have heard from others and from yourself, and from the fact that you are not married yet, though you are as old as I am, I conclude that you don't have marriages among you. Those of you who are already married continue married, but the rest of you do not enter into new relations. You do not take pains to perpetuate the human race. And if there were no other people besides you, the human race would have long ago perished," said Julius, repeating what he had many times heard.

"That is unjust," said Pamphilius. "It is true we do not make it our aim to perpetuate the human race, and we take no anxious care about this, as I have many times heard from your wise men. We take for granted that our Heavenly Father has already provided for this: our aim is simply to live in accordance with His will. If the per-petuation of the race is consonant with His will, then it will be perpetuated; if not, then it will come to an end; this is not our business or our care; our care is to live in accordance with His will. His will is expressed both in our sermons and in our revelation, where it is said that the husband shall cleave unto the wife, and they twain shall be one flesh. Marriage amongst us is not only not forbidden, but is encouraged by our elders and teachers. The difference between marriage amongst us and marriage amongst you consists solely in this: that our law has revealed to us that every one who looks lustfully on a woman commits a sin; and therefore we and our women, instead of adorning ourselves and stimulating lust, try to avoid it as much as possible, so that the feeling of love, like that between brothers and sisters, may be stronger than that of lust, for one woman, which you call love."

"But still you cannot suppress the feeling for beauty," said Julius. "I am convinced, for example, that the beautiful young girl with whom you were carrying grapes, in spite of her garb, which concealed her charming figure, must awaken in you the feeling of love to a woman."

"I do not know as yet," said Pamphilius, reddening. "I have not thought about her beauty. You are the first person that has spoken of it. She is to me only as a sister. But I will continue what I was just going to say to you concerning the difference between our form of marriage and yours. The variance arises from the fact that, among you, lust, under the name of beauty and love and the service of the goddess Venus, is maintained and expressed in men. With us it is the contrary; carnal desire is not regarded as an evil—for God has created no evil—but a good, which becomes an evil when it is not in its place—a temptation, as we call it; and we try to avoid it by all the means in our power. And that is why I am not married as yet, though very possibly I might marry tomorrow."

"But what decides this?"

"The will of God."

"How do you find it out?"

"If one never seeks for its indications, one will never see them; but if one is all the time on the lookout for them, they become clear, as to you omens by sacrifices and birds are clear. And as you have your wise men who interpret for you the will of the gods by their wisdom, and by the vitals of the sacrificed victim, and by the flight of birds, so have we our wise men who explain to us the will of the Father by the revelation of Christ, by the promptings of their hearts, and the thoughts of other men, and chiefly by love to them."

"But all this is very indefinite," objected Julius. "What shows you, for example, when and whom you ought to marry? When I was about to marry, I had a choice between three girls. These girls were selected from the rest because they were beautiful and rich, and my father was satisfied whichever one of them I chose. Out of the three I chose my Eulampia because she was more beautiful and more attractive than the others. But what will govern you in your choice?"

"In order to answer you," said Pamphilius, "I must inform you, first of all, that as according to our doctrine all men are equal before our Father, so likewise they are equal before us both in their station and in their spiritual and physical qualities, and consequently our choice (if I may use this word so meaningless to us) cannot be in any way circumscribed. Any one of all the men and women of the world may be the wife of a Christian man or the husband of a Christian woman."

"That would make it still more impossible to decide," said Julius.

"I will tell you what our elder told me as to the difference between a Christian and a pagan marriage. The pagan—you, for example—chooses a wife who, according to his idea, will cause him, personally, more delight than any one else. In this choice his eyes wander about, and it is hard to decide; the more, because the enjoyment is before him. But the Christian has no such choice; or rather the choice for his personal enjoyment occupies not the first, but a subordinate place. For the Christian the question is whether by his marriage he is going contrary to God's will."

"But in what respect can there be in marriage anything contrary to God's will?"

"I might forget the 'Iliad,' which you and I read together, but you who live amid poets and sages cannot forget it. What is the whole 'Iliad'? It is a story of violations of the will of God in relation to marriage. Menelaus and Paris and Helen and Achilles and Agamemnon and Chreseis—it is all a description of the terrible tribulations that have ensued and are all the time coming from this violation."

"In what consists this violation?"

"It consists in this: that a man loves a woman for the personal enjoyment he gets from connection with her, and not because she is a human being like himself, and so he enters into matrimony for the sake of his pleasure. Christian marriage is possible only when a man has love for his fellow-men, and when the object of his carnal love has already been the object of fraternal love of man to man. As a house can be built satisfactorily and lastingly only when there is a foundation; as a picture can be painted only when there is something prepared to paint it on; so carnal love is lawful, reasonable, and lasting only when it is based on the respect and love of man to man. On this foundation only can a reasonable Christian family life be established."

"But still," said Julius, "I do not see why Christian love, as you call it, excludes such love for a woman as Paris experienced."

"I don't say that Christian marriage did not permit exclusive love for a woman; on the contrary, only then is it reasonable and holy; but exclusive love for a woman can take its rise only when the existent love to all men has not been previously violated. The exclusive love for a woman which the poets sing, calling it good, though it is not founded on love to men, has no right to be called love at all. It is animal passion, and very frequently passes over into hate. The best proof of this is how this so-called love, or *eros,* if it be not founded on brotherly love to all men, becomes brutal; this is shown in the cases where violence is offered to the very woman whom a man professes to love, and in so doing compels her to suffer, and ruins her. In violence it is manifest that there is no love to man—no, not if he torments the one he loves. But in un-Christian marriage violence is often concealed when the man that weds a girl who does not love him, or who loves some one else, compels her to suffer and does not pity her, provided only he satisfies his passion."

"Let us admit that this is so," said Julius, "but if a girl loves him, then there is no injustice, and I don't see any difference between Christian and pagan marriage."

"I do not know the details of your marriage," replied Pamphilius; "but I know that every marriage having for its basis personal advantage only cannot help being the cause of discord, just exactly as the mere act of feeding cannot take place among animals and men without quarrels and brawls. Every one wants the sweet morsel, and since there is an insufficiency of sweet morsels for all, the quarrel breaks out. Even if there is no outward quarrel, there is a secret one. The weak one desires the sweet morsel, but he knows that the strong one will not give it to him, and though he is aware of the impossibility of taking it directly away from the strong one, he looks at him with secret hatred and envy, and seizes the first opportunity of getting it away from him. The same is true of pagan marriages, only it is twice as bad, because the object of the hatred is a man, so that enmity is produced even between husband and wife."

"But how manage so that the married couple love no one but each other? Always the man or the girl is found loving this person or another. And then in your system the marriage is impossible. This is the very reason I see the justice of what is said about you, that you do not marry at all. It is for this reason you are not married, and apparently will not marry. How can it possibly be that a man should marry a single woman never having before kindled the feelings of love in some other woman, or that a girl should reach maturity without having awakened the feelings of some man? How must Helen have acted?"

"The elder Cyril thus speaks in regard to this: in the pagan world, men having no thought of love to their brethren, never having trained that feeling, think about one thing—about the awakening of passionate love toward some woman, and they foster this passion in their hearts. And therefore in their world every Helen, and every woman like Helen, stimulates the love of many. Rivals fight with one another, and strive to supplant one another as animals do to possess the female. And to a greater or less degree their marriage is a constraint. In our community we not only do not think of the personal fascination of beauty, but we avoid all temptations which lead to that, and which in the heathen world are highly regarded as a merit and an object of adoration.

"We, on the contrary, think about those obligations of reverence and love to our neighbors which we have without distinction for all men, for the greatest beauty and the greatest ugliness. We use all our endeavors to educate this feeling, and so in us the feeling of love toward men gets the upper hand of the seduction of beauty, and conquers it, and annihilates the discords arising from sexual relations. The Christian marries only when he knows that his union with a woman causes no one any grief."

"But is this possible?" interrupted Julius. "Can men regulate their inclinations?"

"It is impossible if they have given them free course, but we can keep them from spreading and rising. Take, for example, the relations of a father to his daughter, of a mother to her sons, of brothers and sisters. The mother is to her son, the daughter to her father, the sister to her brother, not an object of personal enjoyment, but of pure love, and the passions are not awakened. They would be awakened only when the father should discover that she whom he had accounted his daughter was not his daughter, or the mother that her son was not her son, or that brother and sister were not brother and sister; but even then this passion would be very feeble and humble, and it would be in a man's power to repress it. The lustful feeling would be feeble, for it would be based on that of maternal, paternal, or fraternal love. Why then can't you believe that the feeling toward all women might be trained and controlled so that they would regard them in the same light as mothers, sisters, and daughters, and that the feeling of conjugal love might grow out of the basis of such an affection? As a brother permits the feeling of love toward the woman whom he has considered his sister to arise only when he has learned that she is not his sister, so when the Christian feels that his love does not injure any one, he permits this passion to arise in his soul."

"Well, but suppose two men love the same girl?"

"Then one sacrifices his happiness to the happiness of the other."

"But supposing she loves one of them?"

"Then the one whom she loves least sacrifices his feelings for the sake of her happiness."

"Well, supposing she loves both, and both sacrifice themselves, whom would she take?"

"In that case the elders would decide the matter, and advise in such a way that the greatest happiness would come to all, with the greatest amount of love."

"But it can't be done in such a way; and the reason is because it is contrary to human nature."

"Contrary to human nature! What is the nature of man? Man, besides being an animal, is a man, and it is true that such a relation to a woman is not consonant with man's animal nature, but is consonant with his rational nature. And when he employs his reason in the service of his animal nature, he does worse than a beast—he descends to violence, to incest—a level to which no brute ever sinks. But when he employs his rational nature to the suppression of the animal, when the animal nature serves, then only he attains the well-being which satisfies him."

5

"But tell me about yourself personally," said Julius. "I see you with that pretty girl; you apparently live near her and serve her; can it be that you do not desire to be her husband?"

"I have not thought about it," said Pamphilius. "She is the daughter of a Christian widow. I serve them just as others do. You ask me if I love her in a way to unite my life with hers. This question is hard for me. But I will answer frankly. This idea has occurred to me; but there is a young man who loves her, and therefore I do not dare as yet to think about it. This young man is a Christian, and loves us both, and I cannot take a step which would hurt him. I live, not thinking about this. I try to do one thing: to fulfil the law of love to men— this is the only thing I demand; I shall marry when I see that it is proper."

"But it cannot be a matter of indifference to the mother whether she has a good industrious son-in-law or not. She would want you, and not any one else."

"No, it is a matter of indifference to her, because she knows that, besides me, all of us are ready to serve her as well as every one else, and I should serve her neither more nor less whether I were her son-in-law or not. If my marriage to her daughter results, I shall enter upon it with joy, and so I should rejoice even if she married some one else."

"That is impossible!" exclaimed Julius. "This is a horrible thing of you—that you deceive yourselves! And thus you deceive others. That stranger told me correctly about you. When I listen to you I cannot help yielding to the beauty of the life which you describe for me; but as I think it over, I see that it is all deception, leading to savagery, brutality, of life approaching that of brutes."

"Wherein do you see this savagery?"

"In this: that as you subject your own lives to labors, you have no leisure or chance to occupy yourselves with arts and sciences. Here you are in ragged dress, with hardened hands and feet; your fair friend, who might be a goddess of beauty, is like a slave. You have no hymns of Apollo, or temples, or poetry, or games—none of those things which the gods have given for beautifying the life of man. To work, work like slaves or like oxen merely for a coarse existence—isn't this a voluntary and impious renunciation of the will and nature of man."

"The nature of man again!" said Pamphilius. "But in what does this nature consist? Is it in this, that you torment your slaves with unbearable labors, that you kill your brothers and reduce them to slavery, and make your women an object of enjoyment? All this is essential for that beauty of life which you consider a part of human nature. Or does it consist in this, that you must live in love and concord with all men, feeling yourself a member of one universal brotherhood?

"You are also greatly mistaken if you think that we scorn the arts and sciences. We highly prize all the qualities with which human nature is endowed. But we look on all the qualities belonging to man as the means for the attainment of one single aim to which we devote our whole lives, and that is to fulfil the will of God. In art and science we do not see an amusement suitable only to while away the time of idle people; we demand from art and science what we demand from all human occupations—that they hold the same activity of love to God and one's neighbor as permeates all the acts of a Christian. We call real science only those occupations which help us to live better, and art we regard only when it purifies our thoughts, elevates our souls, increases the force which we need for a loving, laborious life. Such science, as far as possible, we develop in ourselves and in our children, and such art we gladly cultivate in our free time. We read and study the writings bequeathed to us; we sing songs, we paint pictures, and our songs and paintings encourage our souls and cheer us up in moments of depression. And this is why we cannot approve of the application which you make of the arts and sciences. Your learned men employ their aptitudes and acquirement to the invention of new means of causing evil to men; they perfect the methods of war, in other words, of murder; they contrive new ways of money-making, that is to say, of enriching some at the expense of others. Your art serves for the erection and decoration of temples in honor of your gods, in whom the more cultivated of you have long ago ceased to believe, but belief in whom you inculcate in others, considering that, by such a deception, you keep them under your power. You erect statues in honor of the most powerful and cruel of your tyrants, whom no one respects, but all fear. In your theaters representations are permitted which hold criminal love up to admiration. Music serves for the delectation of your rich men who have eaten and drunken at their luxurious feasts. Pictorial art is employed in representing in houses of debauchery such scenes as no sober man unvitiated by animal passions could look at without blushing. No, not for this was man endowed with these lofty qualities which differentiate him from the beasts! It is impossible to use them for the mere gratification of your bodies. Conse-

those that need may acquire what is required for supporting life. If any one desired to take these grapes away from us we should give them up without resistance. This is the precise reason why we have no fear, even of an invasion of the barbarians. If they proceeded to take from us the products of our toil, we should let them go; if they insisted on our working for them, we should joyfully comply with their demands, and not only would they have no reason to kill us or torture us, but it would be contrary to their interest to do so. The barbarians would speedily understand and like us, and we should have far less to endure at their hands than from the enlightened people that surround us now and persecute us.

"Your accusation against us consists in this—that we do not wholly attain what we are striving for; that is, that we do not recognize violence and private property, and at the same time we take advantage of them. If we are deceivers, then it is no use to talk with us, and we are worthy neither of anger nor of being exposed, but only of scorn, and we should willingly accept your scorn, since one of our rules is the recognition of our insignificance. But if we are genuine in our striving toward what we profess, then your blaming us for deception would be unjust. If we strive, as I and my brethren strive, to fulfil our Teacher's law, then we strive for it, not for external ends— for riches and honors, for you see all these things we do not recognize—but for something else. You are seeking

crating our whole lives to the accomplishment of the will of God, we all the more employ our highest faculties in the same service."

"Yes," said Julius, "all this would be admirable if life in such conditions was possible; but it is not possible to live so. You deceive yourselves. You do not acknowledge our protection. But if it were not for the Roman legions, could you live in any comfort? You profit by our protection, though you do not acknowledge it. Some among you, as you yourself say, protect yourselves. You do not acknowledge private property, but take advantage of it; we have it and give it to you. You yourselves do not give away your grapes, but sell them and then make purchases. All this is a cheat. If you did what you say, then it would be so; but now you deceive others as yourselves."

Julius was indignant, and he spoke out what he had in his mind. Pamphilius was silent and waited his turn. When Julius had finished, Pamphilius said:

"You are wrong in thinking that we do not acknowledge your protection, and yet take advantage of it. Our well-being consists in our not requiring protection, and this cannot be taken away from us. Even if material objects, which constitute property in your eyes, pass through our hands, we do not call them ours, and we give them to whoever needs them for subsistence. We sell goods to those that wish to buy them; yet it is not for the sake of increasing our private means, but solely that

your best advantage, and so are we; the only difference is that we see our advantage in different things. You believe that your well-being consists in riches and honors; we believe in something else. Our belief shows us that our advantage is not in violence, but in submissiveness; not in wrath, but in giving everything away. And we, like plants in the light, cannot help striving in the direction where we see our advantage. It is true we do not accomplish all we wish for our own advantage; but how can it be otherwise? You strive to have the most beautiful woman for a wife, to have the largest property—but have you, or has any one else succeeded in doing this? If the arrow does not hit the bull's-eye, does the bowman any the less cease to aim at it, because he fails many times to hit it? It is the same with us. Our well-being, according to the teaching of Christ, is in love. We search for our advantage, but each one in his own way falls more or less short of attaining it."

"Yes, but why don't you believe in all human wisdom, and why do you turn your back on it, and put your faith in your one crucified Teacher? Your thraldom, your submissiveness before Him, is what repels me."

"Again you make a mistake, and any one makes a mistake who thinks that we, in fulfilling our doctrine, pin our faith to anything because the man we believe in commanded it. On the contrary, those that seek with all their soul for the instructions of Truth, for Communion with the Father, those that seek for true happiness, cannot help hitting upon that path which Christ traversed, and, therefore, cannot help following Him, seeing Him as their leader. All who love God meet on this path, and there you will be also! He is the Son of God and the mediator between God and men, and this is so, not because any one has told us this, and we blindly believe it, but because all those that seek God find His Son before them, and only through Him can they understand, see, and know God."

Julius made no reply to this, and sat for a long while silent.

"Are you happy?" he asked.

"I have nothing better to desire. But although, for the most part, I experience a sense of perplexity, a consciousness of some vague injustice, yet that is the very reason I am so tremendously happy," said Pamphilius, smiling.

"Yes," said Julius; "maybe I should have been happier if I had not met that stranger, and if I had joined you."

"Why! if you think so, what prevents your doing so even now?"

"How about my wife?"

"You say she has an inclination to Christianity, then she will come with you."

"Yes, but we have already begun a different kind of life; how can we break it off? We have begun; we must live it out," said Julius, picturing to himself the dissatisfaction which his father and mother and friends would feel, and, above all, the energy which it would require to make this change.

At this moment there appeared at the door of the shop this young girl, Pamphilius' friend, accompanied by a young man. Pamphilius joined them, and the young man said loud enough for Julius to hear that he had been sent by Cyril to buy leather. The grapes had been sold and wheat had been bought. Pamphilius proposed to the young man to go home with Magdalina while he himself should buy and bring home the leather. "It will be pleasanter for you," said he.

"No, it would be pleasanter for Magdalina to go with you," said the young man, and he took his departure. Julius introduced Pamphilius in the shop to a tradesman whom he know. Pamphilius put the wheat into bags, and bestowing the smaller share on Magdalina, took up his own heavy load, said good-by to Julius, and left the city with the young girl. As he turned into a side street he looked round and nodded his head to Julius, and then still more joyously smiling said something to Magdalina, and thus they vanished from sight.

"Yes, I should have done better if I had gone to them," said Julius to himself, and in his imagination, commingling, arose two pictures: that of the lusty Pamphilius with the tall robust maiden carrying the baskets on their heads and their kindly radiant faces; then that of his own home which he had left that morning, and to which he should return, and then his pampered beautiful wife, of whom he had grown so tired, lying in her finery and bracelets on rugs and cushions.

But Julius had no time to think long; his acquaintances, the tradesmen, came, and they entered upon their usual proceedings, finishing up with a dinner with liquors and the night with women. . . .

6

Ten years passed. Julius saw nothing more of Pamphilius, and his interviews gradually faded from his remembrance, and his impressions of him and the Christian life grew dim.

Julius' life ran in the usual course. About that time his father died, and he was obliged to take the head of the whole business, which was complicated; there were old customers, there were salesmen in Africa, there were clerks, there were debts to be collected and to be paid. Julius, in spite of himself, was drawn into business and gave all his time to it. Moreover, new cares came upon him. He was selected for some civic function. And this new occupation, flattering to his pride, was attractive to him. Besides his commercial affairs, he was also interested in public matters, and having brains and the gift of eloquence, he proceeded to use his influence among his fellow-citizens, so as to acquire a high public position.

In the course of these ten years, a serious and, to him, unpleasant change had also taken place in his family life. Three children had been born to him, and this had estranged him from his wife. In the first place, his wife had lost a large part of her beauty and freshness; in the second place, she paid less attention to her husband. All her affection and tenderness were lavished on the children. Though the children were handed over to nurses and attendants, after the manner of the pagans, Julius often found them in their mother's rooms or found her in theirs. But the children for the most part were a burden to Julius, occasioning him more annoyance than pleasure.

Engrossed in his commercial and public affairs, Julius had abandoned his former dissipated life, but he took it for granted that he needed some refined recreation after his labors, and he did not find it with his wife. At this time she was more and more occupied with a Christian slave-woman, was more and more carried away by the new doctrine, and had renounced everything external and pagan which had constituted a charm for Julius. As he did not find this in his wife, he took up with a woman of frivolous character, and enjoyed with her those leisure moments which remained to him above his duties.

If Julius had been asked whether he was happy or unhappy in these years of his life, he could not have replied.

He was so busy! He hurried from affair to affair, from pleasure to pleasure, but there was not one so satisfying to him that he would have it last. Everything he did was of such a kind that the quicker he got through with it the better he liked it; and none of his pleasures was so sweet as not to be poisoned by something, not to have mingled with it the weariness of satiety.

This kind of existence Julius was leading when an event happened which very nearly revolutionized the whole nature of his life. At the Olympic games he was taking part in the races, and as he was driving his chariot successfully near the goal, he suddenly collided with another which he was just outstripping: the wheel was broken, he was thrown out, and two of his ribs and an arm were fractured. His injuries were serious, but not fatal; he was taken home, and had to lie in bed for three months.

In the course of these three months, in the midst of severe physical sufferings, his thought began to ferment, and he had leisure to review his life as if it were the life of a stranger, and his life presented itself before him in a gloomy light, the more because during this time three unpleasant events, deeply mortifying to him, occurred.

The first was that a slave in whom his father had reposed implicit trust, having gone to Africa for him to purchase precious stones, had run away, causing great loss and confusion in Julius' business.

The second was that his concubine had deserted him, and accepted a new protector.

The third and most unpleasant blow was that during his illness the election for the position of administrator which he had been ambitious to fill, took place, and his rival was chosen. All this, it seemed to Julius, resulted from the fact that his chariot-wheel had swerved to the left the width of a finger.

As he lay alone on his couch, he began involuntarily to think how from such insignificant circumstances his happiness depended, and these ideas led him to still others, and to a recollection of his former misfortunes, of his attempt to join the Christians, and of Pamphilius, whom he had not seen for ten years.

These recollections were still further strengthened by conversations with his wife, who, during his illness, was frequently with him, and told him everything she could learn about Christianity from her slave-woman. This slave-woman had lived for a time in the same community where Pamphilius lived, and knew him. Julius wanted to see this slave-woman, and when she came to his bedside she gave him a circumstantial account of everything, and particularly about Pamphilius.

"Pamphilius," the slave-woman said, "was one of the best of the brethren, and was loved and regarded by them all. He was married to that same Magdalina whom Julius had seen ten years previous. They already had several children. Any man who did not believe that God had created men for their good should go and observe the lives of these," said the slave-woman in conclusion.

Julius dismissed the slave-woman and remained alone, thinking over what he had heard. It made him envious to compare Pamphilius' life with his own, and he tried not to think about it.

In order to divert his mind, he took the Greek manuscript which his wife had put into his hands, and began to read it. In the manuscript he reads as follows:

There are two paths; one of life and one of death. The path of life consists in this; first, thou must love God, who created thee; secondly, thy neighbor as thyself; and do not unto another that which thou wouldst not have done unto thee. The doctrine included in these words is this:

Bless those that curse you;

Pray for your enemies and for your persecutors; for what thanks have you if you love those that love you. Do not even the heathen the same?

Do you love them that hate you and you will not have enemies.

Abstain from sensual and worldly lusts.

If any one smite thee on the right cheek, turn to him the other also; and thou shalt be perfect. If any one compel thee to go one mile with him go with him twain;

If any one take what is thine, ask it not back, since this thou canst not do;

If anyone take away thy outer garment, give also thy shirt;

Give to every one that asketh of thee and demand it not back, since the Father desires that His beneficent gifts be given unto all.

Blessed is he that giveth according to the Commandments.

My child! shun all evil and all appearance of evil. Be not given to wrath, since wrath leadeth to murder; nor to jealousy, nor to quarrelsomeness, since the outcome of all these is murder.

My child! be not lustful, since lust leadeth to fornication; be not obscene, for from obscenity proceedeth adultery.

My child! be not deceitful, because falsehood leadeth to theft; be not mercenary, be not ostentatious, since from all this proceedeth theft.

My child! be not a murmurer, since this leadeth to blasphemy; be not insolent or evil-minded, since from all this cometh blasphemy.

But be meek, for the meek shall inherit the earth.

Be long-suffering and gentle and mild and humble and good, and always beware of the words to which thou lendest thine ear.

Be not puffed up with pride and give not thy soul to insolence.

Yea, verily, let not thy soul cleave to the proud, but treat the just and the peaceful as thy friends.

All things that happen unto thee accept as for thy good, knowing that nothing can befall thee without God.

My child! be not the cause of discord, but act as a peacemaker when men are quarreling.

Widen not thy hands to receive, and make them not narrow when thou givest. Hesitate not about giving; and when thou hast given, do not repine, for thou knowest who is the beneficent giver of rewards.

Turn not from the needy but share all things with thy brother, and call nothing thine own property, for if you are all sharers in the imperishable, then how much more in that which perisheth.

Teach thy children from early youth the fear of God.

Correct not thy man-servant nor thy maid-servant in anger, lest they cease to fear God, who is above you both; for He cometh not to call men, judging by whom they are, but He calleth those whom the Spirit hath prepared.

But the path of Death is this: first of all it is evil and full of curses; here are murder, adultery, lust, fornication, robbery, idolatry, sorcery, poison, rape, false evidence, hypocrisy, duplicity, slyness, pride, wrath, arrogance, greediness, obscenity, hatred, insolence, presumption, vanity; here are the persecutors of the good, haters of the truth, lovers of falsehood, those that do not recognize rewards for justice, that do not cling to the good nor to just judgment, those that are vigilant, not for what is right but for what is wrong, from whom gentleness and patience hold aloof; here are those that love vanity and yearn for rewards, that have no sympathy with their neighbors, that work not for the overworked, that know not their Creator, slaughterers of children, breakers of God's images, who turn from the needy, persecutors of the oppressed, defenders of the rich, lawless judges of the poor, sinners in all things!

Children, beware of all such persons!

Long before he had read the manuscript to the end, Julius had the experience which men always have when they read books—that is to say, the thoughts of others—with a genuine desire for the Truth; he felt that he had entered with his whole soul into communion with the one that had inspired them. He read on and on, his mind foreseeing what was coming; and he not only agreed with the thoughts of the book, but he imagined that he himself had uttered them.

There happened to him that ordinary phenomenon, not noticed by many persons and yet most mysterious and significant, consisting in this, that the so-called living man becomes alive when he enters into communion—unites—with the so-called dead, and lives one life with them.

Julius' soul merged with the one who had written and composed these thoughts, and after this union had taken place he contemplated himself and his life. And he himself and his whole life seemed to him one horrible mistake. He had not lived, but by all his labors in regard to life, and by his temptations, he had only destroyed in himself the possibility of a true life.

"I do not wish to destroy life; I wish to live, to go on the path of life," he said to himself.

He remembered all that Pamphilius had said to him in their former interviews, and it seemed to him now so clear and indubitable that he was amazed that he could ever have believed in the stranger, and have renounced his intention of going to the Christians. He remembered also what the stranger had said to him:

"Go when you have had experience of life."

"Well, I have had experience of life, and found nothing in it."

He also remembered how Pamphilius had said to him that whenever he should come to them they would be glad to receive him.

"No, I have erred and suffered enough," he said to himself. "I will renounce everything, and I will go to them and live as it says here."

He communicated his plan to his wife, and she was delighted with his intention. She was ready for everything. The only thing left was to decide how to carry it into execution. What should they do with the children? Should they take them along or leave them with their grandmother? How could they take them? How, after the tenderness of their nurture, subject them to all the trials of an austere life? The slave-woman proposed to accompany them. But the mother was troubled about her children, and declared that it would be better to leave them with their grandmother, and go alone. And they both decided to do this.

All was determined, and nothing but Julius' illness prevented its fulfilment.

7

In this condition of mind Julius fell asleep. The next morning he was told that a skillful physician traveling through the city desired to see him, and promised to give him speedy relief. Julius with joy received the physician. He proved to be none other than the stranger whom Julius had met when he started to join the Christians.

After he had examined his wounds, the physician prescribed certain simples for renewing his strength.

"Shall I be able to work with my arm?" asked Julius.

"Oh, yes, to drive a chariot, or to write; yes."

"But I mean hard work—to dig?"

"I was not thinking about that," said the physician, "because such work is not necessary to one in your position."

"On the contrary, it is very necessary to me," said Julius; and he told the physician that since the time he had last seen him he had followed his advice, had made trial of life, but life had not given him what it had promised him, but, on the contrary, had disillusioned him, and that he now was going to carry out the plan of which he had spoken to him at that time.

"Yes, evidently they have put into effect all their powers of deception and entangled you, if you, in your position, with your responsibilities, especially in regard to your children, cannot see their fallacies."

"Read this," was all that Julius said, producing the manuscript he had been reading. The physician took the manuscript and glanced at it.

"I know this," said he; "I know this fraud, and I am surprised that such a clever man as you are can fall into such a snare."

"I do not understand you. Where lies the snare?"

"The whole thing is in life; and here these sophists and rebels against men and the gods propose a happy path of life in which all men would be happy; there would be no wars, no executions, no poverty, no licentiousness, no quarrels, no evil. And they insist that such a condition of men would come about when men should fulfil the precepts of Christ; not to quarrel, not to commit fornication, not to blaspheme, not to use violence, not to bear ill-will against one another. But they make a mistake in taking the end for the means. Their aim is to keep from quarreling, from blasphemy, from fornication, and the life, and this aim is attained only by means of social life. And in speaking thus they say almost what a teacher of archery should say, if he said, 'You will hit the target when your arrow flies in a straight line directly to the target.'

"But the problem is, how to make it fly in a straight line. And this problem is solved in archery by the string being tightly stretched, the bow being elastic, the arrow straight. The same with the life of men;—the very best life for men—that in which they need not quarrel, or commit adultery, or do murder—is attained by the bowstring—the rulers; the elasticity of the bow—the force of the authorities; and the straight arrow—the equity of the law. But they, under the guise of living a better life, destroy whatever has improved or is improving it. They acknowledge no rulers, no authority, no laws."

"But they claim that even without rulers, authorities and laws human life will be vastly better if men would only fulfil the law of Christ."

"Yes, but what guarantee have we that men will fulfil that law? Absolutely none! They say: 'You have made trial of life without authorities and laws, and it has always been a failure. Try it now without authorities and laws, and you will soon see it becoming perfect. You cannot deny this, not having tested it by experience.' Here the sophistry of these impious men becomes evident. Are they more logical than the farmer who says: 'You sow the seed in the ground, and then cover it up with soil, and yet the crop falls far below your desires. My advice is: sow it in the sea, and the result will be far more satisfactory. And do not attempt to deny this theory. You cannot do so, never having tested it by experience.'"

"Yes, that's true," said Julius, who was beginning to waver.

"Not only this," continued the physician, "let us admit what is senseless, what is impossible—let us admit that the foundations of this Christian doctrine may be communicated to all men, like a dose of certain drops, and that suddenly all men should fulfil Christ's teachings, love God and their fellows, and fulfil the precepts. Let us admit this, and yet the way of life, according to their teaching, would not bear examination. There would be no life, and life would be cut short. Now the living live out their lives, but their children will not live their full time, or not one in ten will. According to their teaching all children must be the same to all mothers and fathers, theirs and others'. How will their children protect themselves when we see that all the passion, all the love, which the mother feels for these children scarcely protects them from destruction? What then will it be when this mother-passion is translated into a general commiseration, the same for all children? Who will take and protect the child? Who will spend sleepless nights watching with sick, ill-smelling children, unless it be the mother? Nature made a protective armor for the child in the mother's love; they take it away, giving nothing in its place. Who will educate the boy? Who will penetrate into his soul, if not his father? Who will ward off danger? All this is put aside! All life that is the perpetuation of the human race is put aside."

"That seems correct," said Julius, carried away by the physician's eloquence.

"No, my friend, have nothing to do with this nonsense, and live rationally; especially now, when such great, serious, and pressing responsibilities rest upon you. To fulfil them is a matter of honor. You have lived to reach your second period of doubt, but go onward, and your doubts will vanish. Your first and indubitable obligation is to educate your children, whom you have neglected; your obligation toward them is to make them worthy servants of their country. The existent form of government has given you all you have: you ought to serve it yourself and to give it capable servants in your children, and by so doing you confer a blessing on your children. The second obligation upon you is to serve the public. Your lack of success has mortified and discouraged you—this circumstance is temporary. Nothing is given to us without effort and struggle. And the joy of triumph is mighty only when the battle was hard. Begin a life with a recognition of your duty, and all your doubts will vanish. They were caused by your feeble state of health. Fulfil your obligations to the country by serving it, and by educating your children for this service. Put them on their feet so that they may take your place, and then calmly devote yourself to that life which attracts you; till then you have no right to do so, and if you did, you would find nothing but disappointment."

8

Either the learned physician's simples or his advice had their effect on Julius: he very speedily recovered his spirits, and his notions concerning the Christian life seemed to him idle vaporings.

The physician, after a visit of a few days, took his departure. Soon after, Julius got up, and, profiting by his advice, began a new life. He engaged tutors for his children, and he himself superintended their instruction. His time was wholly spent in public duties, and very soon he acquired great consideration in the city.

Thus Julius lived a year, and during this year not once did he remember the Christians. But during this time a tribunal was appointed to try the Christians in their city. An emissary of the Roman Empire had come to Cilicia to stamp out the Christian faith. Julius heard of the measures taken against the Christians, and though he supposed that it concerned the Christian community in which Pamphilius lived, he did not think of him. But one day as he was walking along the square in the place where his official duties called him, he was accosted by a poorly dressed, elderly man, whom he did not recognize at first. It was Pamphilius. He came up to Julius, leading a child by the hand.

"How are you, friend?" said Pamphilius. "I have a great favor to ask of you, but I don't know as you will be willing to recognize me as your friend, now that we Christians are being persecuted; you might be in danger of losing your place if you had any relations with me."

"I am not in the least afraid of it," replied Julius, "and as a proof of it I will ask you to come home with me. I will even postpone my business in the market so as to talk with you and be of service to you. Let us go home together. Whose child is this?"

"It is my son."

"Really, I need not have asked. I recognize your features in him. I recognize also those blue eyes, and I should not have to ask who your wife is: she is the beautiful woman whom I saw with you some years ago."

"You have surmised correctly," replied Pamphilius. "Shortly after we met, she became my wife."

The friends went to Julius' home. Julius summoned his wife and gave the boy to her, and brought Pamphilius to his luxurious private room.

"Here you can say anything; no one will hear us," said Julius.

"I am not afraid of being heard," replied Pamphilius; "since my request is not that the Christians, who have been arrested, may not be sentenced and executed, but only that they may be permitted publicly to confess their faith."

And Pamphilius told how the Christians arrested by the authorities had sent word to the community from the dungeons where they were confined. The elder Cyril, knowing of Pamphilius' relations with Julius, commissioned him to go and plead for the Christians. The Christians did not ask for mercy. They considered it their mission to bear witness to the truth of Christ's teaching. They could bear witness to this in the course of a long life of eighty years, and they could bear witness to the same by enduring tortures. Either way was immaterial to them; and physical death, unavoidable as it was, for them was alike free from terror and full of joy, whether it came immediately or at the end of half a century: but they wished their lives to be useful to men, and therefore they had sent Pamphilius to labor in their behalf, that their trial and punishment might be public.

Julius was dumfounded at Pamphilius' request, but he promised to do all in his power.

"I have promised you my intercession," said Julius, "but I have promised it to you on account of my friendship for you, and on account of the peculiarly pleasant feeling of tenderness which you have always awakened in me; but I must confess that I consider your doctrine most senseless and harmful. I can judge in regard to this, because not very long ago, in a moment of disappointment and illness, in a state of depression of spirits, I once more shared your views, and once more almost abandoned everything and went to you. I understand on what your error is based, for I have been through it; it is based on selfishness, on weakness of spirit, and the feebleness caused by ill health; it is a creed for women, but not for men."

"Why so?"

"Because although you acknowledge the fact that discord and violence are a part of human nature, you do not wish to take part in that violence or to teach others to do so. And without taking your share of the burden you nevertheless take advantage of the organization of society, which is based on violence. Do you call that fair? The world has always existed by means of its rulers: they assume the responsibility of governing, they protect us from enemies, domestic and foreign. We subjects, in return for this, pay the rulers deference and homage, obey their commands, and assist them by serving the State when we are needed. But you, out of pride, instead of taking part by your labors in the affairs of the empire, and in proportion to your services rising higher and higher in the estimation of men, you forthwith, by your pride, I say, regard all men as equal, so that you consider no one higher than yourselves, and consider yourselves equal to Cæsar.

"You yourself think so, and teach others to think so. And for the weak and the lazy this is a great temptation. Instead of laboring, every slave immediately counts himself equal to Cæsar. If men listened to you, society would be dissolved, and we should return to primitive savagery. You in the empire preach the dissolution of empire. But your very existence is dependent on the empire. If it was not for that, you would not be. You would all be slaves of the Scythians or the barbarians, the first who knew of your condition. You are like a tumor destroying the body, but able to make a show, and to feed on the body and nothing else. And the living body struggles with it and suppresses it! Thus do we act in regard to you, and we cannot do otherwise. And notwithstanding my promise to help you, and to comply with your request, I look on your doctrine as most harmful and low: low, because dishonorably and unjustly you devour the breast that nourishes you: take advantage of the blessings of the imperial order without sharing in its support, and yet trying to destroy it!"

"What you say would be just," said Pamphilius, "if we really lived as you think. But you do not know about our life, and you have formed a false conception of it. For you, with your habitual luxury, it is hard to imagine how little a man requires when he exists without superfluities. A man is so constituted that, when he is well, he can produce with his hands far more than he needs for the support of his life. Living in a community as we do, we are able by our labor to support without effort our children, and the aged and the sick and the feeble. You assert that we Christians arouse in the slave the desire to be the Cæsar; on the contrary, both by word and deed we fulfil one thing: patient submissiveness and work, the most humble work of all—the work of the working-man. We know nothing and we care nothing about affairs of state. We know one thing, but we know it beyond question— that our well-being is only when the well-being of others is found, and we strive after this well-being; the well-being of all men is in their union. And union is attained not by violence, but by love. The violence of a brigand is as atrocious as is that of troops against their enemies, or of the judge against the culprit, and we can have no part in either. Nor can we profit by the work of others enforced by violence. Violence is reflected on us, but we do not inflict it, our share consists in submitting to it without protest."

"Yes," said Julius, "you preach love, but the result of your preaching is savagery, retrogression to primitive conditions of murder, robbery, and every kind of violence, which according to your doctrine must not be repressed in any way."

"No, that's not true," said Pamphilius, "and if you will examine the results of our teaching and the example of our lives you will see that they do not lead to murder, robbery and violence. On the contrary, those crimes can only be opposed by the means we practice. They existed long before Christianity and men found no way of coping with them. When violence meet violence, crimes are not checked but are provoked, because feelings of anger and bitterness are aroused.

"Look at the mighty Roman Empire, where legislation has been raised to a science, and the laws are thoroughly studied and administered, and the office of judge is highly regarded. Nevertheless debauchery and crime are everywhere prevalent. In the early days, when laws were not so numerous or so carefully administered, there was a higher standard of virtue; but simultaneously with the study and application of the laws there has been going on in the Roman empire a steady deterioration of morals, accompanied by a vast increase in the number and variety of criminal offenses. Nor can it be otherwise. The only way to grapple with such crimes and with evil is the Christian way of love. The heathen weapons of vengeance, punishment and violence are inefficacious. All the preventive and remedial laws and punishments in the world will fail to eradicate people's propensities to do wrong. The root of evil must be got at, which is in the heart of man. That is what we aim at, while you try to repress the outward manifestations of evil. Not looking for its source and not knowing where it is, you can never hope to find it.

"Most crimes are perpetrated by men who desire to get more of this world's good than they can rightfully acquire. Some of these—as, for instance, monstrous commercial frauds—are perpetrated under the protection of the law, and those that are punishable are so cleverly managed that they often escape the penalty. Christianity removes all incentive to such crimes, because those that practice it refuse to take more than what is strictly needed for the support of life, and thereby give up to others their free labor. So that the sight of accumulated wealth is not a temptation, and those that are driven to desperation by hunger find what they need without having to use violent means of obtaining it. Some criminals avoid us altogether. Others join us and gradually become useful workers.

"As regards the crimes provoked by the play of passions: jealousy, carnal love, anger, and hatred. Laws never suppress such crimes. Obstacles only make them worse. But Christianity teaches men to curb their passions by a life of love and labor, so that the spiritual principle will overcome the fleshly. And as Christianity spreads, the number of crimes of this sort will diminish.

"There is still another class of crimes, which have their root in a sincere desire to help humanity. The wish to alleviate the sufferings of an entire people will impel certain men called revolutionists to kill a tyrant with the notion that they are benefiting a majority. The origin of such crimes is a mistaken conviction that evil may be done in order that good may follow. Crimes of this description are not lessened by laws against them, they are provoked by them. The men that commit crimes of this kind have a noble motive—a desire to do good to others. Most men of this kind, though mistaken in their hopes and beliefs, are impelled by the noble motive of desire to do good and they are ready to sacrifice their lives and all they have, and no danger or difficulty stands in their way. Punishment cannot restrain them. Danger only gives them new life and spirit. If they suffer, they are regarded as martyrs, and earn the sympathy of mankind, and they stimulate others to go and do likewise. We see this in the history of all nations. We Christians, though we clearly perceive the error of such conspirators, appreciate their sincerity and self-denial. But we believe that evil will only disappear when men understand the misery that results from it both for themselves and for others. Brotherhood can only be attained when we are all brothers.

"You may decide for yourself which of us—we Christians or you Romans—is more successful in the struggle with crime: we Christians, who preach and prove the joy and delight of a spiritual life, from which no evil can arise; or you Roman rulers and judges, who pass sentence according to the letter of a dead law and thus lash your victims into fury and drive them to the utmost hatred?"

"As long as I keep listening to you," said Julius, "I seem to get the impression that your point of view is correct. But tell me, Pamphilius, why are people against you? Why do they hunt you down and kill you? Why does your teaching of love lead to discord?"

"The reason for this is not in us but outside of us. Above and beyond the temporary laws established by the State and recognized by all men, there are eternal laws engraved in the hearts of men. We Christians obey these universal laws, discerning in the life of Christ their clearest and fullest expression, and condemning, as a crime, every form of violence which transgresses His commandments. We feel bound to observe the civil laws of the country in which we live, unless these laws are opposed to God's laws. 'Render unto Cæsar the things that are Cæsar's, and unto God the things that are God's.' We Christians strive to do away with all crimes, both those against the State and those that go counter to God's will, and, therefore, our fight with crime is more comprehensive than that carried on by the State. But this recognition of God's will as the highest law offends those that claim precedence for a private law, or that take some ingrained custom of their class as law. Such men are animated by feelings of enmity for those that proclaim that man has a higher mission than to be merely subjects of a State or members of a Society. It was of such that Christ said: 'Woe unto you, Pharisees! for ye take away the key of knowledge: ye enter not in yourselves, and them that are entering in ye hinder.'

"We have no enmity towards any man, not even against those that persecute us, and our way of life injures no man. The only reason why men hate and persecute us is that our way of life is a constant rebuke to those whose conduct is based on violence. We have not the power of stopping this hostility, which does not have its source in us, because we cannot cease to realize that truth which we have accepted, because we cannot live contrary to our conscience and reason. In regard to this very hostility which our faith should arouse in others against us, our Teacher said, 'Think not that I am come to send peace into the world; I came not to send peace, but a sword.'

"Christ experienced this hostility in His own life-time and more than once he warned us, His disciples, in regard to it. 'Me,' He said, 'the world hateth because its deeds are evil. If ye were of the world the world would love you, but since ye are not of this world therefore the world hateth you, and the time will come when he who killeth you will think he is serving God.' But we, like Christ, 'fear not them which kill the body but are not able to kill the soul. And this is their condemnation, that light is come into the world, and men loved darkness rather than light because their deeds were evil.'

"In this there is nothing to worry over, because the truth will prevail. The sheep hear the shepherd's voice, and follow him because they know his voice. And Christ's flock will not perish but will increase, attracting to it new sheep from all the lands of the earth, for 'The wind bloweth where it listeth and thou hearest the sound thereof, but canst not tell whence it cometh and whither it goeth . . .'"

"Yes," Julius said, interrupting him, "but are there many sincere ones among you? You are often blamed for only pretending to be martyrs and glad to lay down your lives for the truth, but the truth is not on your side. You are proud madmen, destroying the foundations of social life."

Pamphilius made no reply, and looked at Julius with melancholy.

9

Just as Julius was saying this, Pamphilius' little son came running into the room, and clung to his father. In spite of all the blandishments of Julius' wife, he would not stay with her, but ran to his father. Pamphilius sighed, caressed his son, and stood up; but Julius detained him, begging him to stay and talk some more, and have dinner with them.

"It surprises me that you are married and have children," exclaimed Julius. "I cannot comprehend how you Christians can bring up children when you have no private property. How can the mothers live in any peace of mind knowing the precariousness of their children's position?"

"Wherein are our children more precariously placed than yours?"

"Why, because you have no slaves, no property. My wife was greatly inclined to Christianity; she was at one time desirous of abandoning this life, and I had made up my mind to go with her. But what chiefly prevented was the fear she felt at the insecurity, the poverty, which threatened her children, and I could not help agreeing with her. This was at the time of my illness. All my life seemed repulsive to me, and I wanted to abandon everything. But then my wife's anxiety, and, on the other hand, the explanation of the physician who cured me, convinced me that the Christian life, as led by you, is impossible, and not good for families; but that there is no place in it for married people, for mothers with children; that in life as you understand it, life—that is the human race—would be annihilated. And this is perfectly correct. Consequently the sight of you with a child especially surprised me."

"Not one child only. At home I left one at the breast and a three-year-old girl."

"Explain to me how this happens. I don't understand. I was ready to abandon everything and join you. But I had children, and I came to the conclusion that, however pleasant it might be for me, I had no right to sacrifice my children, and for their sake I continued to live as before, in order to bring them up in the same conditions as I myself had grown up and lived."

"Strange," said Pamphilius; "we take diametrically opposite views. We say: 'If grown people live a worldly life it can be forgiven them, because they are already corrupted; but children! That is horrible! To live with them in the world and tempt them! 'Woe unto the world because of offenses, for it must needs be that offenses come; but woe to that by whom the offense cometh.'

"So spake our Teacher, and I do not say this to you as a refutation, but because it is actually so. The chiefest obligation that we have to live as we do arises from the fact that amongst us are children—those beings of whom it is said, 'Except ye become as little children ye shall not enter into the Kingdom of Heaven.'"

"But how can a Christian family do without definite means of subsistence?"

"According to our faith there is only one means of subsistence—loving labor for men. For your means of livelihood you depend on violence. It can be destroyed as wealth is destroyed, and then all that is left is the labor and love of men. We consider that we must hold fast by that which is the basis of everything, and that we must increase it. And when this is done, then the family lives and prospers.

"No," continued Pamphilius; "if I were in doubt as to the truth of Christ's teaching, and if I were hesitating as to the fulfilling of it, then my doubts and hesitations would instantly come to an end if I thought about the fate of children brought up among the heathen in those conditions in which you grew up, and are educating your children. Whatever we, a few people, should do for the arrangement of our lives, with palaces, slaves, and the imported products of foreign lands, the life of the majority of men would still remain what it must be. The only security of that life will remain, love of mankind and labor. We wish to free ourselves and our children from these conditions, not by love, but by violence. We compel men to serve us, and—wonder of wonders!—the more we secure, as it were, our lives by this, the more we deprive ourselves of the only true, natural, and lasting security—love. The same with the other guarantee—labor. The more a man rids himself of labor and accustoms himself to luxury, the less he becomes fitted for work, the more he deprives himself of the true and lasting security. And these conditions in which men place their children they call *security!* Take your son and mine and send them now to find a path, to transmit an order, or to do any needful business, and see which of the two would do it most successfully; or try to give them to be educated, which of the two would be most willingly received? No, don't utter those horrible words that the

Christian life is possible only for the childless. On the contrary, it might be said: to live the pagan life is excusable only in those who are childless. 'But woe to him who offendeth one of these little ones.'"

Julius remained silent.

"Yes," said he, "maybe you are right, but the education of my children is begun, the best teachers are teaching them. Let them know all that we know. There can be no harm in that. But for me and for them there is still time. They may come to you when they reach their maturity, if they find it necessary. I also can do this, when I set them on their feet and am free."

"Know the Truth and you shall be free," said Pamphilius. "Christ gives full freedom instantly; earthly teaching never will give it. Good-by."

And Pamphilius went away with his son.

The trial was public, and Julius saw Pamphilius there as he and other Christians carried away the bodies of the martyrs. He saw him, but as he stood in fear of the authorities he did not go to him, and did not invite him home.

10

Twenty years more passed. Julius' wife died. His life flowed on in the labors of his public office, in efforts to secure power, which sometimes fell to his share, sometimes slipped out of his grasp. His wealth was large, and kept increasing.

His sons had grown up, and his second son, especially, began to lead a luxurious life. He made holes in the bottom of the bucket in which the wealth was held, and in proportion as the wealth increased, increased also the rapidity of its escape through these holes.

Julius began to have just such a struggle with his sons as he had had with his father—wrath, hatred, jealousy.

About this time a new prefect deprived Julius of his favor.

Julius was forsaken by his former flatterers, and banishment threatened him. He went to Rome to offer explanations. He was not received, and was ordered to depart.

On reaching home he found his son carousing with boon companions. The report had spread through Cilicia that Julius was dead, and his son was celebrating his father's death! Julius lost control of himself, struck his son so that he fell, apparently lifeless, and he went to his wife's room. In his wife's room he found a copy of the gospel, and read:

Come unto me all ye that labor and are heavy laden and I will give you rest. Take my yoke upon you and learn of me, for I am meek and lowly of heart, and ye shall find rest unto your souls. For my yoke is easy and my burden is light.

"Yes," said Julius, to himself, "He has been calling me long. I did not believe in Him, and I was disobedient and wicked; and my yoke was heavy and my burden was grievous."

Julius long sat with the gospel opened on his knee, thinking over his past life and recalling what Pamphilius had said to him at various times.

Then Julius arose and went to his son. He found his son on his feet, and was inexpressibly rejoiced to find he had suffered no injury from the blow he had given him. Without saying a word to his son, Julius went into the street and bent his steps in the direction of the Christian settlement. He went all day, and at eventide stopped at a countryman's for the night. In the room which he entered lay a man. At the noise of steps the man roused himself. It was the physician.

"No, this time you do not dissuade me!" cried Julius. "This is the third time I have started *thither,* and I know that there only shall I find peace of mind."

"Where?" asked the physician.

"Among the Christians."

"Yes, maybe you will find peace of mind, but you will not have fulfilled your obligations. You have no courage. Misfortunes have conquered you. True philosophers do not act thus. Misfortune is only the fire in which the gold is tried. You have passed through the furnace, and now you are needed, you are running away. Now test others and yourself. You have gained true wisdom, and you ought to employ it for the good of your country. What would become of the citizens if those that knew men, their passions and conditions of life, instead of devoting their knowledge and experience to the service of their country, should hide them away, in their search for peace of mind. Your experience of life has been gained in society, and so you ought to devote it to the same society."

"But I have no wisdom at all. I am wholly in error. My errors are ancient, but no wisdom has grown out of them. Like water, however old and stale it is, it never becomes wine."

Thus spake Julius; and seizing his cloak, he left the house and, without resting, walked on and on. At the end of the second day he reached the Christians.

They received him joyfully, though they did not know that he was a friend of Pamphilius, whom every one loved and respected. At the refectory Pamphilius recognized his friend, and with joy ran to him, and embraced him.

"Well, at last I have come," said Julius. "What is there for me to do? I will obey you."

"Don't worry about that," said Pamphilius. "You and I will go together."

And Pamphilius led Julius into the house where visitors were entertained, and showing him a bed, said:

"In what way you can serve the people you yourself will see after you have had time to examine into the way we live; but in order that you may know where immediately to lend a hand, I will show you something tomorrow. In our vineyards the grape harvest is taking place. Go and help there. You yourself will see where there is a place for you."

The next morning Julius went to the vineyard. The first was a young vineyard hung with thick clusters. Young people were plucking and gathering them. All the places were occupied, and Julius, after going about for a long while, found no chance for himself.

He went farther. There he found an older plantation; there was less fruit, but here also Julius found nothing to do; all were working in pairs, and there was no place for him.

He went farther, and came to a superannuated vineyard. It was all empty. The vinestocks were gnarly and crooked, and, as it seemed to Julius, all empty.

"Just like my life," he said to himself. "If I had come the first time it would have been like the fruit in the first vineyard. If I had come when the second time I started, it would have been like the fruit in the second vineyard; but now here is my life; like these useless superannuated vinestocks, it is good only for fire-wood."

And Julius was terrified at what he had done; he was terrified at the punishment awaiting him because he had ruined his life. And Julius became melancholy, and he said: "I am good for nothing; there is no work I can do now."

And he did not rise from where he sat, and he wept because he had wasted what could never more return to him. And suddenly he heard an old man's voice—a voice calling him. "Work, my brother," said the voice. Julius looked around and saw a white-haired old man, bent with years, and scarcely able to walk. He was standing by a vinestock and gathering from it the few sweet bunches remaining. Julius went to him.

"Work, dear brother; work is joyous;" and he showed him how to find the bunches here and there.

Julius went and searched; he found a few, and brought them and laid them in the old man's basket. And the old man said to him:

"Look, in what respect are these bunches worse than those gathered in yonder vineyards? 'Walk while ye have the light, lest darkness come upon you,' said our Teacher. 'And this is the will of Him that sent me; that every one which seeth the Son and believeth on Him, may have everlasting life, and I will raise him at the last day.

"'For God sent not His Son into the world to condemn the world; but that the world through Him might be saved.

"'He that believeth on Him is not condemned: but he that believeth not is condemned already, because he hath not believed in the name of the only begotten Son of God.

"'And this is the condemnation, that light is come into the world, and men loved darkness rather than light because their deeds were evil.

"'For every one that doeth evil hateth the light, neither cometh to the light lest his deeds should be reproved.

"'But he that doeth truth cometh to the light, that his deeds may be made manifest that they are wrought in God.'

"Be not unhappy, my son. We are all the children of God and His servants. We all go to make up His one army! Do you think that He has no servants besides you? And that if you, in all your strength, had given yourself to His service, would you have done all that He required all that men ought to do to establish His kingdom? You say you would have done twice, ten times, a hundred times more than you did. But suppose you had done ten thousand times ten thousand more than all men, what would that have been in the work of God? Nothing! To God's work, as to God Himself, there are no limits and no end. God's work is in you. Come to Him, and be not a laborer but a son, and you become a copartner with the infinite God and in His work. With God there is neither small nor great, but there is straight and crooked. Enter into the straight path of life and you will be with God, and your work will be neither small nor great, but it will be God's work. Remember that in heaven there is more joy over one sinner, than over a hundred just men. The world's work, all that you have neglected to do, has only shown you your sin, and you have repented. And as you have repented, you have found the straight path;

go forward in it with God, and think not of the past, or of great and small. Before God, all living men are equal. There is one God and one life."

And Julius found peace of mind, and he began to live and to work for the brethren according to his strength. And he lived thus in joy twenty years longer, and he did not perceive how he died the physical death.

1893

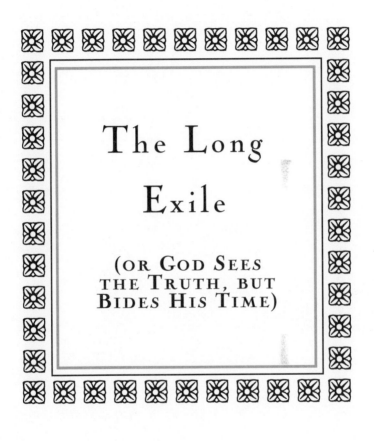

The Long Exile

(OR GOD SEES THE TRUTH, BUT BIDES HIS TIME)

Once upon a time there lived in the city of Vladimir a young tradesman named Aksenof. He had two shops and a house.

Aksenof had a ruddy complexion and curly hair; he was a very jolly fellow and a good singer. When he was young he used to drink too much, and when he was tipsy he was turbulent; but after his marriage he ceased drinking, and only occasionally had a spree.

One summer Aksenof was going to Nizhni to the great Fair. As he was about to bid his family good-by, his wife said to him:

"Ivan Dmitrievitch, do not start today; I dreamed that some misfortune befell you."

Aksenof laughed at her, and said:

"Are you still afraid that I shall go on a spree at the Fair?"

His wife said:

"I myself know not what I am afraid of, but I had such a bad dream; you seemed to be coming home from town, and you took off your hat, and I looked, and your head was all gray."

Aksenof laughed.

"That means good luck. See, I am going now. I will bring you some rich remembrances."

And he bade his family farewell and set off.

When he had gone half his journey, he fell in with a tradesman who was an acquaintance of him, and the two stopped at the same tavern for the night. They took tea together, and went to sleep in adjoining rooms.

Aksenof did not care to sleep long; he awoke in the middle of the night, and in order that he might get a good start while it was cool he aroused his driver and bade him harness up, went down into the smoky hut, settled his account with the landlord, and started on his way.

After he had driven forty versts,[1] he again stopped to get something to eat; he rested in the vestibule of the inn, and when it was noon, he went to the doorstep and ordered the samovar[2] got ready; then he took out his guitar and began to play.

Suddenly a troïka[3] with a bell dashed up to the inn, and from the equipage leaped an official with two soldiers; he came directly up to Aksenof, and asked:

"Who are you? Where did you come from?"

Aksenof answered without hesitation, and asked him if he would not like to have a glass of tea with him.

But the official kept on with his questions:

"Where did you spend last night? Were you alone or with a merchant? Have you seen the merchant this morning? Why did you leave so early this morning?"

Aksenof wondered why he was questioned so closely; but he told everything just as it was, and asked:

"Why do you put so many questions to me? I am not a thief or a murderer. I am on my own business; there is nothing to question me about."

Then the official called up the soldiers, and said:

"I am the police inspector, and I have made these inquiries of you because the merchant with whom you spent last night has been stabbed. Show me your things, and you men search him."

They went into the tavern, brought in the trunk and bag, and began to open and search them. Suddenly the police inspector pulled out from the bag a knife, and demanded:

"Whose knife is this?"

Aksenof looked, and saw a knife covered with blood taken from his bag, and he was frightened.

"And whose blood is that on the knife?"

Aksenof tried to answer, but he could not articulate his words:

"I . . . I . . . don't . . . know . . . I . . . That knife . . . it is . . . not mine. . . ."

Then the police inspector said:

"This morning the merchant was found stabbed to death in his bed. No one except you could have done it. The tavern was locked on the inside, and there was no one in the tavern except yourself. And here is the bloody knife in your bag, and your guilt is evident in your face.

Tell me how you killed him and how much money you took from him."

Aksenof swore that he had not done it, that he had not seen the merchant after he had drunk tea with him, that the only money that he had with him—eight thousand rubles—was his own, and that the knife was not his.

But his voice trembled, his face was pale, and he was all quivering with fright, like a guilty person.

The police inspector called the soldiers, and commanded them to bind Aksenof, and take him to the wagon.

When they took him to the wagon with his feet tied, Aksenof crossed himself and burst into tears.

They confiscated Aksenof's things and his money, and took him to the next city, and threw him into prison.

They sent to Vladimir to make inquiries about Aksenof's character, and all the merchants and citizens of Vladimir declared that Aksenof, when he was young, used to drink and was wild, but that now he was a worthy man. Then he was brought up for judgment.

He was sentenced for having killed the merchant and for having robbed him of twenty thousand rubles.

Aksenof's wife was dumfounded by the event, and did not know what to think. Her children were still small, and there was one at the breast. She took them all with her and journeyed to the city where her husband was imprisoned.

At first they would not grant her admittance, but afterward she got permission from the nachalniks and was taken to her husband.

When she saw him in his prison garb, in chains, together with murderers, she fell to the floor, and it was a long time before she recovered from her swoon. Then she placed her children around her, sat down amid them, and began to tell him about their domestic affairs, and to ask him about everything that had happened to him.

He told her the whole story.

She asked:

"What is to be done now?"

He said:

"We must petition the Tsar. It is impossible that an innocent man should be condemned."

The wife said that she had already sent in a petition to the Tsar, but that the petition had not been granted. Aksenof said nothing, but was evidently very much downcast.

Then his wife said:

"You see the dream I had, when I dreamed that you had become gray-headed, meant something, after all. Already your hair has begun to turn gray with trouble. You ought to have stayed at home that time."

And she began to tear her hair, and she said:

"Vanya, my dearest husband, tell your wife the truth: Did you commit that crime?"

Aksenof said:

"So you, too, have no faith in me!"

And he wrung his hands and wept.

Then a soldier came and said that it was time for the wife and children to go. And Aksenof for the last time bade his family farewell.

When his wife was gone, Aksenof began to think over all that they had said. When he remembered that his wife had also distrusted him, and had asked him if he had murdered the merchant, he said to himself:

"It is evident that no one but God can know the truth of the matter, and He is the only one to ask for mercy, and He is the only one from whom to expect it."

And from that time Aksenof ceased to send in petitions, ceased to hope, and only prayed to God. Aksenof was sentenced to be knouted, and then to exile with hard labor.

And so it was done.

He was flogged with the knout, and then, when the wounds from the knout were healed, he was sent with other exiles to Siberia.

Aksenof lived twenty-six years in the mines. The hair on his head had become white as snow, and his beard had grown long, thin, and gray. All his gayety had vanished. He was bent, his gait was slow, he spoke little, he never laughed, and he spent much of his time in prayer.

Aksenof had learned while in prison to make boots, and with the money that he earned he bought the "Book of Martyrs," and used to read it when it was light enough in prison, and on holidays he would go to the prison church, read the Gospels, and sing in the choir, for his voice was still strong and good.

The authorities liked Aksenof for his submissiveness, and his prison associates respected him and called him "Grandfather" and the "man of God." Whenever they had petitions to be presented, Aksenof was always chosen to carry them to the authorities; and when quarrels arose among the prisoners, they always came to Aksenof as umpire.

Aksenof never received any letters from home, and he knew not whether his wife and children were alive.

One time some new convicts came to the prison. In the evening all the old convicts gathered around the newcomers, and began to ply them with questions as to the cities or villages from which this one or that one had come, and what their crimes were.

At this time Aksenof also was sitting on his bunk, near the strangers, and, with bowed head, was listening to what was said.

One of the new convicts was a tall, healthy-looking old man of sixty years, with a close-cropped gray beard. He was telling why he had been arrested. He said:

"And so, brothers, I was sent here for nothing. I unharnessed a horse from a postboy's sledge, and they caught me with it, and insisted that I was stealing it. But I said, 'I only wanted to go a little faster, so I whipped up the horse. And, besides, the driver was a friend of mine. Its' all right,' I said. 'No,' said they; 'you were stealing it.' But they did not know what and where I had stolen. I have done things which long ago would have sent me here, but I was not found out; and now they have sent me here without any justice in it. But what's the use of grumbling? I have been in Siberia before. They did not keep me here very long, though." . . .

"Where did you come from?" asked one of the convicts.

"Well, we came from the city of Vladimir; we are citizens of that place. My name is Makar, and my father's name was Semyon."

Aksenof raised his head and asked:

"Tell me, Semyonuitch, have you ever heard of the Aksenofs, merchants in Vladimir city? Are they alive?"

"Indeed, I have heard of them! They are rich merchants, though their father is in Siberia. It seems he was just like any of the rest of us sinners. And now tell me, grandfather, what you were sent here for?"

Aksenof did not like to speak of his misfortunes; he sighed, and said:

"Twenty-six years ago I was condemned to hard labor on account of my sins."

Makar Semyonof said:

"But what was your crime?"

Aksenof replied, "So I must have deserved this."

But he would not give any further particulars; the other convicts, however, related why Aksenof had been sent to Siberia. They told how on the road some one had killed a merchant, and put the knife into Aksenof's luggage, and how he had been unjustly punished for this.

When Makar heard this, he glanced at Aksenof, slapped himself on the knees, and said:

"Well, now, this is wonderful! This is really wonderful! You have been growing old, grandfather!"

They began to ask him what he thought was wonderful, and where he had seen Aksenof. But Makar did not answer; he only repeated:

"A miracle, boys! how wonderful that we should meet again here!"

And when he said these words, it came over Aksenof that perhaps this man might know who had killed the merchant. And he said:

"Did you ever hear of that crime. Semyonuitch, or did you ever see me before?"

"Of course I heard of it! The country was full of it. But it happened a long time ago. And I have forgotten what I heard," said Makar.

"Perhaps you heard who killed the merchant?' asked Aksenof.

Makar laughed, and said:

"Why, of course the man who had the knife in his bag killed him. It would have been impossible for any one to put the knife in your things and not have been caught doing it. For how could the knife have been put into your bag? Was it not standing close by your head? And you would have heard it, wouldn't you?"

As soon as Aksenof heard these words he felt convinced that this was the very man who had killed the tradesman. He stood up and walked away. All that night he was unable to sleep. Deep melancholy came upon him, and he began to call back the past in his imagination.

He imagined his wife as she had been when for the last time she had accompanied him to the Fair. She seemed to stand before him exactly as if she were alive, and he saw her face and her eyes, and he seemed to hear her words and her laugh.

Then his imagination brought up his children before him; one a boy in a little fur coat, and the other at his mother's breast.

And he imagined himself as he was at that time, young and happy. He remembered how he had sat on the steps of the tavern when they arrested him, and how he had played on his guitar, and how his soul was full of joy at that time.

And he remembered the place of execution where they had flogged him, and the executioner, and the people standing around, and the chains and the convicts, and all his twenty-six years of prison life, and he remembered his old age.

And such melancholy came upon Aksenof that he was tempted to put an end to himself.

"And all on account of this criminal!" said Aksenof to himself.

And then he began to feel such anger against Makar Semyonof that he almost lost himself, and was crazy with desire to pay off the load of vengeance. He repeated prayers all night, but could not recover his calm. When day came, he walked by Makar and did not look at him.

Thus passed two weeks. At night Aksenof was not able to sleep, and such melancholy had come over him that he did not know what to do.

One time during the night, as he happened to be passing through the prison, he saw that the soil was disturbed under one of the bunks. He stopped to examine it. Suddenly Makar crept from under the bunk, and looked at Aksenof with a startled face.

Aksenof was about to pass on so as not to see him, but Makar seized his arm, and told him how he had been digging a passage under the wall, and how every day he carried the dirt out in his boot-legs and emptied it in the street when they went out to work. He said:

"If you only keep quiet, old man, I will get you out too. But if you tell on me, they will flog me; but afterward I will make it hot for you. I will kill you."

When Aksenof saw the man who had injured him, he trembled all over with rage, twitched away his arm, and said:

"I have no reason to make my escape, and to kill me would do no harm; you killed me long ago. But as to telling on you or not, I shall do as God sees fit to have me."

On the next day, when they took the convicts out to work, the soldiers discovered where Makar Semyonof had been digging in the ground; they began to make a search, and found the hole. The chief came into the prison and asked every one, "Who was digging that hole?"

All denied it. Those who knew did not name Makar, because they were aware that he would be flogged half to death for such an attempt.

Then the chief came to Aksenof. He knew that Aksenof was a truthful man, and he said:

"Old man, you are truthful; tell me before God who did this."

Makar Semyonof was standing near, in great excitement, and he looked at the nachalnik, but he dared not look at Aksenof.

Aksenof's hands and lips trembled, and it was some time before he could speak a word. He said to himself:

"If I shield him ... but why should I forgive him when he has been my ruin? Let him pay for my sufferings! But shall I tell on him? They will surely flog him. But what difference does it make what I think of him? Will it be any the easier for me?"

Once more the chief demanded:

"Well, old man, tell the truth! Who dug the hole?"

Aksenof glanced at Makar Semyonof, and then said:

"I cannot tell, your honor. God does not bid me tell. I will not tell. Do with me as you please; I am in your power."

In spite of all the chief's efforts, Aksenof would say nothing more. And so they failed to find out who dug the hole.

On the next night, as Aksenof was lying on his bunk, and was almost asleep, he heard some one come along and sit down at his feet.

He peered through the darkness and saw that it was Makar. Aksenof asked:

"What do you wish of me? What are you doing here?"

Makar Semyonof remained silent. Aksenof arose, and said:

"What do you want? Go away, or else I will call the guard."

Makar Semyonof bent close to Aksenof, and said in a whisper:

"Ivan Dmitrievitch, forgive me!"

Aksenof said:

"What have I to forgive you?"

"I killed the merchant and put the knife in your bag. And I was going to kill you too, but there was a noise in the yard; I thrust the knife in your bag, and slipped out of the window."

Aksenof said nothing, and he did not know what to say. Makar got down from the bunk, knelt on the ground, and said:

"Ivan Dmitrievitch, forgive me, forgive me for God's sake. I will confess that I killed the merchant—they will pardon you. You will be able to go home."

Aksenof said:

"It is easy for you to say that, but how could I endure it? Where should I go now? . . . My wife is dead! my children have forgotten me. . . . I have nowhere to go." . . .

Makar did not rise; he beat his head on the ground, and said:

"Ivan Dmitritch, forgive me! When they flogged me with the knout, it was easier to bear than it is now to look at you. . . . And you had pity on me after all this . . . you did not tell on me. . . . Forgive me for Christ's sake! Forgive me, though I am a cursed villain!"

And the man began to sob.

When Aksenof heard Makar Semyonof sobbing, he himself burst into tears, and said:

"God will forgive you; maybe I am a hundred times worse than you are!"

And suddenly he felt a wonderful peace in his soul. And he ceased to mourn for his home, and had no desire to leave the prison, but only thought of his last hour.

Makar Semyonof would not listen to Aksenof, and confessed his crime.

When the orders came to let Aksenof go home, he was dead.

c. 1872

Notes

1. Nearly twenty-six and a half miles.
2. Water-boiler for making Russian tea.
3. A team of three horses harnessed abreast; the outside two gallop, the shaft-horse trots.

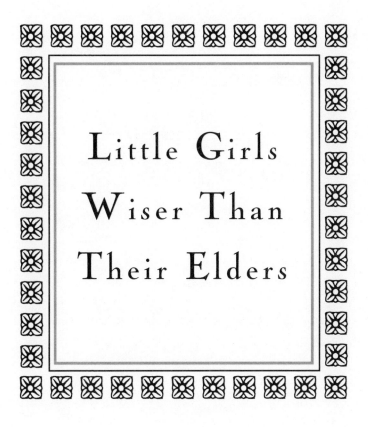

Little Girls
Wiser Than
Their Elders

aster was early. Folks had just ceased going in sledges. The snow still lay in the courtyards, and little streams ran through the village. In an alley between two dvors a large pool had collected from the dung-heaps. And near this pool were standing two little girls from either dvor—one of them younger, the other older.

The mothers of the two little girls had dressed them in new sarafans—the younger one's blue, the elder's of yellow flowered damask. Both wore red handkerchiefs. The little girls, after mass was over, had gone to the pool, shown each other their dresses and begun to play. And the whim seized them to splash in the water. The younger one was just going to wade into the pool with her little slippers on; but the older one said:

"Don't do it, Malashka . . . your mother will scold. I'm going to take off my shoes and stockings . . . you take off yours."

The little girls took off their shoes and stockings, held up their clothes, and went into the pool so as to meet. Malashka waded in up to her ankles, and said:

"It's deep, Akulyushka[1] . . . I am afraid."

"Nonsense! It won't be any deeper. Come straight toward me."

They approached nearer and nearer to each other. And Akulka said:

"Be careful, Malashka, don't splash, but go more slowly."

But the words were hardly out of her mouth, when Malashka put her foot down into the water; it splashed directly on Akulka's sarafan. The sarafan was well spattered, and the water flew into her nose and eyes.

Akulka saw the spots on her sarafan; she became angry with Malashka, scolded her, ran after her, tried to slap her.

Malashka was frightened when she saw what mischief she had done; she sprang out of the pool, and hastened home.

Akulka's mother happened to pass by and saw her little daughter's sarafan spattered, and her shirt bedaubed.

"How did you get yourself all covered with dirt, you good-for-nothing?"

"Malashka spattered me on purpose."

Akulka's mother caught Malashka, and struck her on the back of the head.

Malashka howled along the whole street. Malashka's mother came out:

"What are you striking my daughter for?"

She began to scold her neighbor. A word for a word; the women got into a quarrel. The muzhiks hastened out, a great crowd gathered on the street. All were screaming. No one would listen to any one. They quarreled, and the

one jostled the other; there was a general row imminent:
but an old woman, Akulka's grandmother, interfered.

She came out into the midst of the muzhiks, and began
to speak.

"What are you doing, neighbors? What day is it? We
ought to rejoice. And you are doing such wrong things!"

They did not heed the old woman; they almost struck
her. And the old woman would never have succeeded in
persuading them, had it not been for Akulka and Malashka. While the women were keeping up the quarrel,
Akulka cleaned her sarafanchik, and came out again to
the pool in the alley. She picked up a little stone, and
began to clear away the earth by the pool, so as to let the
water run into the street.

While she was cleaning it out, Malashka also came
along and began to help her—to make a little gutter with
a splinter.

The muzhiks were just coming to blows when the
water reached the street, flowing through the gutter made
by the little girls; and it went straight to the very spot
where the old woman was trying to separate the muzhiks.

The little girls were chasing it, one on one side, the
other on the other, of the runnel.

"Hold it back, Malashka! hold it!" cried Akulka. Malashka also tried to say something, but she laughed so
that she could not speak.

Thus the little girls were chasing it, and laughing as the splinter swam down the runnel.

They ran right into the midst of the muzhiks. The old woman saw them, and she said to the muzhiks:

"You should fear God, you muzhiks! It was on account of these same little girls that you picked a quarrel, but they forgot all about it long ago; dear little things, they are playing together lovingly again."

The muzhiks looked at the little girls, and felt ashamed. Then the muzhiks laughed at themselves, and went home to their dvors.

"If ye are not like little children, ye cannot enter into the kingdom of God."

1885

Notes

1. Akulka and Akulyushka, diminutives of Akulina.